Tell Tail Clues

Gayle Roper

AnniesFiction.com

Books in the Aspen Falls Mysteries series

Foal Me Once
Dogged Deception
Tell Tail Clues
The Claus Will Come Out

... and more to come!

Tell Tail Clues
Copyright © 2022 Annie's.

The characters and events in this book are fictional, and any resemblance to actual persons
or events is coincidental.

Library of Congress-in-Publication Data
Tell Tail Clues / by Gayle Roper
p. cm.
I. Title
              2021948826

AnniesFiction.com
(800) 282-6643
Mysteries of Aspen Falls™
Series Creator: Shari Lohner
Series Editor: Elizabeth Morrissey
Cover Illustrator: Gregory Copeland

10 11 12 13 14 | Printed in China | 9 8 7 6 5 4 3 2

1

With a coordinated lift, a bit of awkward shuffling, and a final push, Dr. Ashley Hart and her friend Holly Kipp maneuvered the bulky printer box out of the electronics store cart and into the back of Ashley's Subaru Outback.

"Oof. Glad that's done." Ashley brushed a stray strand of dark blonde hair toward her ponytail. "Thanks so much for your help, Holly."

"My pleasure, although I'm sure you could have managed." Holly grinned, her dark eyes sparkling. "I can't blame you for wanting company, though."

"Friends make boring jobs like printer shopping much more fun," Ashley agreed. "I didn't expect mine to break, and I can't keep using the printer at work."

"Ryan says keeping work and personal stuff separate is important, especially for tax purposes," Holly said, her eyes lighting at the mention of her husband. Ryan was an accountant who kept the books for Holly's pet grooming service, 3 Alarm Fur, and Ashley's veterinary practice, Happy Tails, which were in the same repurposed firehouse in downtown Aspen Falls, Colorado.

Ashley checked her watch. "Speaking of Ryan, what time does he expect you home?"

"Don't worry about him." Holly shook her head, sending her auburn-threaded black waves bouncing. "I'm sure he's lost track of time watching the Broncos game."

"Is there anyone in Colorado who doesn't love that football team?"

Ashley leaned forward and checked the gray sky. "I wonder if it's going to snow."

Holly studied the sky, pierced by the granite spears of the Rocky Mountains. "Could be."

"You've lived in Colorado your whole life. You're supposed to be able to tell."

Holly shrugged. "The weather still manages to surprise me on occasion."

"It's barely November, and it's already snowed five times."

"You're not in Ohio anymore." Holly grinned.

"You can say that again." Ashley had been born and raised in Dayton, attended veterinary school in Columbus, and worked at a chain clinic there for several years before taking a leap of faith and moving to Colorado to open her own practice.

"It's better than Oz, though. The Munchkins didn't have the beautiful Rocky Mountains lining the Yellow Brick Road."

Ashley laughed. "I'm the lucky one, then. The scenery here always brings me joy. I can't believe I get to live in such a beautiful place."

"You made the right decision moving here," Holly said. "And not just because you met me."

Ashley chuckled in agreement, then they climbed into the Outback and set off for Aspen Falls, which was about half an hour away. A few gentle flakes hit the windshield as they rounded a curve on their way back to Ashley's newly adopted hometown, and she grinned.

"Max loves snow." She pictured her Dalmatian with a huge doggie smile. "Especially sticking his nose in and burrowing."

"As you might expect from a Labrador, Zeus likes to eat it," Holly said. "And roll in it. And leap in the air and catch snowballs. I think he muddles through summer because he knows winter's coming."

Just ahead, a fancy gilded sign that read *Marley Meadows Ranch and Kennel* announced a nice-size spread that Ashley knew well. The property was home not only to the kennel and a small ranch that boarded horses and taught horsemanship, but it was also the residence of a world-famous occupant, Sweetbriar's Lady Fair. The national champion Cavalier King Charles spaniel lovingly known as Sweetie was one of Ashley's favorite patients, and Sweetie's owner, Kristin Holmes, was quickly becoming a good friend.

"How are Sweetie's puppies doing?" Holly asked as they passed the ranch. "I bet they're the cutest things ever."

"They are." Ashley pictured the little bundles of fur pushing their greedy ways to their mom for dinner, not caring in the least that they were being fed by a national treasure. "Three are tricolored like their father, which means they're black and white with brown eyebrows. Three are brown and white Blenheims like Sweetie, and one is ruby, all rich brown with red overtones."

"Do any of them have the right markings for the show ring?"

"For color, a couple are promising, especially one of the tricolors. As for the show ring, it's personality matched with beauty that makes all the difference. Sweetie has personality oozing from every little furry inch."

"And the looks to back it up. Any of the pups show personality yet?"

Ashley laughed, recalling her last visit. "There's definitely an alpha who beats everyone to supper. The rest squirm their way more temperately. I'll be stopping by tomorrow for a wellness visit. Ask me afterward."

"Make sure you take pictures," Holly said. "I can't wait to see them."

"Will do," Ashley promised. "Who knows, maybe one of them will be as famous as Sweetie one day."

"Speaking of famous, did you know Kristin's kids—the real

children, not the furry ones—are already as well-known as Sweetie?"

"Really?" Ashley glanced at the Marley Meadows sign in her rearview mirror. "Why?"

"They're online influencers."

"So they have lots of followers on social media and make money off of sponsorships and advertising?"

Holly nodded. "They've both got thousands of followers for dog-related content. Rani's business is called Rani A.'s Dog Duds Designs, though she shortens it to Dog Duds for the most part. She designs and sells dog clothes all over the world."

"Does she make them herself?"

"Some, and it's the ones she makes that are in demand and for a very nice price. She's quite clever with both her designs and her sewing machine. It's become prestigious in certain circles to have a Dog Duds outfit for your dog, especially since a picture of a TV actress with her Pekingese in a Dog Duds raincoat and boots appeared in a Hollywood magazine. Rani now has advertisers who pay to be on her site or in the videos she posts of her creative process."

"Wow." Ashley was impressed. "What kind?"

"Dog food manufacturers, grooming supplies, and mass-market dog clothing. I hear she makes a very tidy income. Pretty impressive for a seventeen-year-old."

Ashley blinked. "When I was seventeen, I was cleaning cages at the local animal shelter."

"You should have taken up sewing. Apparently, it's lucrative."

Ashley laughed. "Anything's more lucrative than volunteer work. And what does Rani's brother do?"

"Garrett makes videos of himself playing with dogs, showing them doing tricks and chasing balls and stuff while he tells facts about that particular breed."

Ashley raised an eyebrow. "Aren't there lots of sites that share information like that?"

Holly shrugged. "Not with owners who resemble a singer in a boy band. Cute, charming, dimples. It's made him a small fortune."

"I never realized videos of guys playing with dogs could be so profitable."

"Well, you're not a teenage girl whose heart melts at the sight of a cute guy wrestling with an adorable puppy. Garrett has basically monetized his chief asset—his looks."

"What happens when he grows out of the teen heartthrob stage?"

"That's a very good question," Holly said. "In the meantime, people love to have their dogs be part of the kids' programs. I've groomed several dogs before a taping. Owners who come into the salon consider it an honor. 'Did you know Scooter is going to model the cutest outfit on *Dog Duds*?' or maybe 'Annie's going to be the featured Yorkie on *Puppy Love.*'"

"How did the kids get started with their shows?" Ashley asked.

Holly's tone became somber. "I think they started filming each other doing silly kid things as a way to deal with their father's death. When they were making videos, they could laugh and have fun. They eventually created their own channels, which turned into brands, and they were off. The rest, as they say, is history."

"How long ago did their father die?"

"About six years ago. Brain aneurysm."

"They were so young." Ashley's heart hurt for the teenagers. "Good for them, making something so successful out of a tough situation."

"I'll send you links so you can check out their content." Holly tapped on her phone. "Especially Rani. Her dog clothes are amazing."

"Thanksgiving's a couple of weeks away. Think she'll sell lots of Pilgrim outfits for dogs?"

"With hats," Holly said with a grin.

"I wonder if I could get Max to wear a Pilgrim hat, or maybe one of those big collars." The thought of her Dalmatian's reaction to such an outfit made her smile. Max was a talker, and he'd make his feelings known.

"Zeus likes costumes. He's very laid-back."

Ashley pictured the chocolate Lab. "Your Zeus is one of the most relaxed dogs I've ever met."

"Zeus is the bes—" Holly broke off with a scream. "Ashley, watch out!"

2

A car parked half on the road had come into view as Ashley rounded a curve. She stomped on the brake pedal, her heart jumping into her throat.

The other car's driver side door hung open. There was no way she could stop in time.

Instinctively, Ashley accelerated and swerved into the other lane, praying that she wouldn't slam into someone driving toward her. An oncoming truck was visible in the distance, so Ashley pressed harder on the gas pedal and zoomed forward.

She gripped the steering wheel, her heart pounding against her ribs. She felt separated from reality, the slow-motion participant in a time-warped event. The Outback flew past the parked car, and Ashley swerved back into her own lane with a second to spare before she would have crashed into the fast-approaching truck.

Trying to still the internal shaking that rippled through her, she slowed until she could pull off the road and fully onto the shoulder. She came to a full stop and sat, hands still gripping the wheel, heart beating madly. Silence rang in her ears.

She took a deep breath and forced her fingers to release the wheel. She glanced at her friend. "Are you okay, Holly?"

Holly sat frozen, her face pale and her eyes wide. Slowly, she relaxed and shifted in her seat to peer through the rear window. "What was that guy thinking, leaving his car right there?"

"I don't know." Now that the tingle of shock all over her body was beginning to recede, Ashley felt an adrenaline-stoked tide of anxiety flood her. She threw open her door and climbed out on shaky legs.

Holly emerged from the car as well, her cell phone to her ear. "I'm calling 911." When the call connected, her voice shook slightly as she spoke to the dispatcher. "We just rounded a curve outside Aspen Falls and found a car blocking the road."

Ashley felt slightly better knowing the police would arrive soon. In the meantime, she walked toward the car to see if anyone was inside. As she reached the vehicle, she peeked through the passenger window and scanned the gray sedan's interior, but it was empty.

"It's abandoned," she called to Holly, who nodded and passed that information on.

Ashley circled the car. The biggest immediate problem was the wide-open driver's door. If she closed it, most of the danger for cars whizzing by would be gone. She hesitated, though. Why was the door open?

Checking for traffic and glad it was a slow Sunday, she hustled into the road and pushed the door closed. It didn't quite catch, but that didn't matter much. At least it was no longer blocking the lane.

She and Holly met on the shoulder, then retreated a few yards so they wouldn't be in danger if a passing car did happen to hit the sedan.

Ashley considered the curve that had blocked the car from view until it was too late. "If someone knew to slow down, they could pass without going too far into the oncoming lane. But they'd have to know to slow, or they'll swerve wide like I did."

"Do you have anything we can put out to warn people?" Holly asked.

"As a matter of fact, I do." Ashley began jogging to the hatch of her car. "When I moved here, my dad bought me an elaborate safety kit, convinced I was going to need it on the 'dangerous mountain roads.'" A retired mechanical engineer, Russ Hart was nothing if not practical.

Ashley lifted the hatch and pulled the kit forward from where it had slid against the back of the rear seat. She opened it and withdrew a set of plastic reflective triangles that measured about a foot high. She grabbed them and ran along the shoulder, past the abandoned car and around the curve. She set the triangles several feet apart, hoping they would do the job of slowing down oncoming cars, then jogged back to Holly and the abandoned car.

"It's a rental." Holly pointed through the passenger window. "I checked the glove compartment and found a packet of paperwork."

Ashley peered in the windows. "Did you see a briefcase or wallet—anything that might hold some kind of ID?"

Holly shook her head. "No. That would be too easy."

"There's a little dirt on the mat on the driver's side."

"I noticed that, but it's dirt like you'd find all over the area." Holly sighed. "Well, it's a mystery. An abandoned car on a road that leads nowhere but Aspen Falls."

A police car appeared from around the bend, passed them, and parked in front of Ashley's Outback. As Officer Wendy Heath climbed out, she put on her police hat over her red hair, and snow immediately dusted it. Moving with an athlete's ease, she joined Ashley and Holly. Her green eyes missed nothing as she scanned the scene. "What have we here?"

Ashley explained about rounding the curve and finding the car with the door open.

"I appreciate the traffic warning triangles you put out," Officer Heath said. "I'd have taken the curve at normal speed if I hadn't seen them."

"I'm surprised you didn't come from town," Holly said.

"I was on a wellness check for an older lady whose family couldn't reach her on the phone," the officer explained. "She lives out past the Weathersby farm."

"I hope she's okay," Ashley said.

"She's fine." Officer Heath laughed. "She's been watching a marathon of a TV series that has her so entranced she's not answering on purpose. She says she's tired of her daughter always telling her what to do."

"Don't you love families?" Holly grinned. Her own family, parents Javier and Elena Morales and teen sisters Maya and Zoe, lived about an hour away in Gilmore Creek. The close-knit clan kept their internal drama to a minimum. Ryan's mom, on the other hand, was one of nine children and often called Ryan and Holly from Arizona with fresh tales of familial discord.

Officer Heath gestured toward her cruiser. "I've got some flares I'm going to put out as a warning. You can pick up your triangles."

"What about the missing driver?" Ashley asked.

"I'll call in a couple of other officers and we'll search the area," the officer assured her. "If we can't find the driver quickly and we think there's really a life-threatening situation, we'll call in Search and Rescue. Once you get your triangles, you ladies are free to go."

After the officer grabbed the flares from her patrol car, Ashley followed her down the road, collecting the triangles as the officer left the more effective flares. Minutes later, she and Holly climbed back into Ashley's Outback and started on their way.

"And Ryan thought this would be a boring trip for a printer." Holly shook her head. "Wait until I tell him about our little mystery."

"Now it's Officer Heath's mystery," Ashley said.

But she spoke too soon. About a mile down the road, just before the massive canyon-spanning bridge that led into Aspen Falls, they rounded another curve and saw a somewhat older man bent double, staggering along the road's edge.

"Goodness!" Ashley slowed. "Let's ask him if we can help."

"Do you think he's the guy from the car?" Holly lowered her window as they pulled up beside the man. "Can we help, sir? Do you need a doctor?"

The man turned their way, his eyes glazed with pain and full of fear. His arms were wrapped around his middle. He gasped for air. "Help." It was a barely audible whimper.

Ashley quickly pulled over, then she and Holly climbed out of the car. As they approached the man, he lost his balance and went down on one knee.

"Call 911 again," Ashley told Holly. She was a veterinarian, not a human doctor, but she hoped her medical training would be of use to the poor suffering man.

As Ashley laid a hand on his shoulder, he gazed up at her from his knees, his distress clear. He gasped, gave a little groan, and toppled the rest of the way to the ground as if he could no longer resist gravity. He lay on his side, curled like a comma. He shuddered as he tried to draw in air.

Ashley dropped to her knees beside him and grabbed his wrist. She felt for a pulse and found a weak, thready one. He was having alarming difficulty drawing a breath. It was as if his lungs were giving out and he had to force them to perform what was supposed to be an automatic function.

Holly knelt beside Ashley and leaned toward the man. "Hold on, sir. An ambulance is coming."

The man's eyes slid closed, and Ashley feared he'd stopped breathing. He gasped and curled more tightly into himself, his arms once again about his middle. It was obvious he was in agony. But what had caused it?

His eyes flew open, and he stared at Ashley. "Danesle see skits," he whispered.

She leaned closer. "What?"

"Danesle see skits."

Those were his final words. With a last gasp, he died.

3

Ashley and Holly stayed a few feet from the man, waiting for Officer Heath a second time. Snow fell softly around them.

They'd covered him with a fleece blanket Ashley carried in her car. She didn't know about Holly, but she felt hollow and helpless inside. The man had needed her, and she hadn't been able to help him despite administering CPR for several minutes. She knew it wasn't her fault he had died. Whatever had killed him had taken effect well before she and Holly came upon him. Still, she swallowed sorrow at his lost life. Did he have a family somewhere waiting for him to come home?

They stood when Officer Heath pulled up and climbed out of her cruiser. Before addressing the women, the policewoman walked to the body, crouched, and checked for signs of life. She stood with a groan. She studied the shrouded figure for a moment, giving him the honor of her full attention, then became all business. She strode toward Ashley and Holly, moving with an authority that made her seem taller than she was.

"You could have waited in the car." The officer pointed to Ashley's Outback. "You didn't have to stay out in the weather."

Ashley shivered and dug her hands deeper into her jacket pockets. "Sitting inside warm and dry seemed disrespectful somehow."

Holly nodded. "He's lying in the snow."

A small smile of understanding quirked Officer Heath's lips. "Tell me what happened."

"Not much to tell." Ashley glanced at Holly, who nodded agreement. She began with their first glimpse of the staggering man and finished with, "And then he looked at me and said, 'Danesle see skits.'"

Heath wrinkled her brow. "What does that mean?"

"I have no idea," Ashley said. "We've been going over and over the words since Holly called it in."

"You heard it too?" the officer asked Holly.

"I did," Holly agreed, "but I heard it as dane slesee skits."

"It doesn't make sense, whichever it is." Ashley spread her hands and shook her head. "He could hardly get any words out."

Officer Heath took out a notepad and wrote the words, pausing a couple of times as she tried to figure out the best way to spell them. "What do you think he was trying to tell you?"

Ashley shrugged. "I don't know. I've never seen him before."

"Have you, Holly?" the officer asked.

"I didn't recognize him," Holly answered. "I don't think he's from around here."

Officer Heath eyed her with interest. "Why do you say that?"

"His car's a rental. I checked the glove compartment." Holly reddened, as if she'd done something she shouldn't.

Heath scanned the surroundings. "I don't see a car."

Ashley frowned. "I figured he goes with the abandoned car."

"Could be," the officer said. "Let's go back to his last words. 'Danesle see skits' or 'Dane slesee skits.' At least you agree that it ended with 'skits.' Like little plays?"

Ashley felt a snowflake tunnel down the neck of her coat. She shuddered and pulled her collar closer. "That's what it sounded like."

An ambulance pulled up, and a man and a woman jumped out. Officer Heath left Ashley and Holly and hurried to meet the first responders. Another cruiser arrived and parked behind the ambulance, and soon the lane heading toward Aspen Falls was cordoned off and full of flashing lights. Flares signaled caution to traffic in both directions, and a uniformed officer stood ready to direct anyone driving by.

The temperature fell as the sun dipped below the mountains, the day being one of the shortest of the year in their little valley due to the angle of the sun and the topography of the peaks. Ashley and Holly huddled together, waiting for permission to leave.

A car appeared from the direction of Aspen Falls and stopped on the side of the road. Ryan Kipp climbed out, scanning the growing mass of people for his wife. He pushed his glasses up on his nose as if that would help him see her. The last ray of sun caught his auburn hair and burnished it copper.

"Ryan!" Holly called, taking a few steps toward him.

He heard and ran in her direction. When they met, he threw his arms around her and held her tight. Ashley watched with a small smile. The longer she knew Holly, the more she appreciated Ryan. Maybe someday someone would love Ashley herself like that. After all, Ryan had chosen to miss the end of the Broncos game to come be with Holly. If that wasn't a sign of true devotion, Ashley didn't know what was.

The couple separated and, holding hands, walked to Ashley.

"Are you okay, Ashley?" Ryan asked.

Ashley warmed at the concern in his hazel eyes. "We've had quite an afternoon."

Another car pulled over and parked, and a tall, dark-haired man climbed out. He paused to survey the scene, then was approached by an officer who—if hand gestures were any indication—wanted him to leave. He shook his head and, seeing Ashley, Holly, and Ryan, pointed in their direction, then loped toward them without waiting for the officer's permission.

As he approached their little group, Ashley felt a wave of relief wash over her. She had to admit to being a bit shaken up by the events of the day. After all, almost crashing into a car, then a truck, hearing a man's final words, and watching him die were each traumatic events on their own. Experienced all within half an hour, they were overwhelming to say the least.

She was proud that neither she nor Holly had fallen to pieces. They'd done all the right things and contacted all the right people. They'd managed well without Ryan or the man walking toward them, but it was nice to have someone concerned enough to come make sure she was okay.

She wanted to lean into the newcomer the way Holly leaned into Ryan, but she knew she couldn't. Theirs was too new a friendship. Still, his presence steadied her.

You're a strong, independent woman, she told herself. But even strong, independent women appreciated a six-foot pillar of strength, especially one as handsome as Ranger Cole Hawke of the White River National Forest.

He stopped in front of Ashley. "I saw you and Holly out here while I was driving home from a hike. I wanted to make sure you were okay."

Ashley's heart gave a little jump at his words, then she warmed at the concern in his eyes.

Officer Heath approached. "You folks don't have to hang around any longer. We know where to find you if we want to clarify anything. Ashley and Holly, you need to stop at the station and make official statements, but tomorrow will be soon enough."

"Will do." Ashley shivered, more than ready to get out of the weather. The slam of the ambulance doors drew her attention, and she thought of the man inside. "Do you know who he is? Er . . . was?"

"His wallet has a driver's license in the name of Edward Warner from Denver," the officer reported. "Does the name mean anything to any of you?"

They all shook their heads.

"I was concerned that he might have ingested a poison," Ashley said. "I know I deal with it in animals, not humans, but the symptoms would be much the same, with the stomach cramps and his difficulty breathing."

Officer Heath eyed her with respect. "They're transporting him to the El Paso County Coroner's Office in Colorado Springs where they have forensic toxicologists who will determine what happened."

"I'm glad they're so dedicated to finding out what happened to him," Cole said. "That's quite a drive from here, especially in this weather."

The ambulance drove off into the growing dusk, this time without lights flashing. There was no longer a need for speed. Officer Heath nodded goodbye, and Ashley, Holly, Ryan, and Cole walked toward their cars.

Holly stepped away from her husband. "Let me get my purse from your car, Ashley, and then I'll go home with Ryan."

Once Holly had retrieved her purse, Ashley gave her a quick hug before she went on her way. As Holly drove off with Ryan, Ashley felt her absence. Having her friend beside her had made the whole ordeal so much more bearable. Now alone, she could feel a delayed reaction setting in.

"Why don't I follow you home?" Cole suggested. "Just to make sure you're okay."

She hoped her relief at not yet being alone wasn't too obvious. "That'd be great." She smiled, thinking of something else he might be willing to do. "Would you mind helping me carry in my new printer? I could probably manage on my own, but it'd be easier with two people."

He smiled. "I'd be glad to help."

She climbed into her car and started for home, his headlights in her rearview a comfort. She loved her log house, which was in a woodsy neighborhood on the edge of Aspen Falls. With its open floor plan, comfortable decor, and big windows offering views of the majestic mountains, it was all she could have asked for. She needed its welcoming warmth tonight.

And Cole's company would be an added reassurance that life was returning to normal. No more almost accidents. No more dead bodies. Just a warm home and a good friend.

She navigated onto her driveway and into her detached two-car garage, and he parked his black Nissan Rogue behind her in the driveway. She walked to the back of the car, where Cole joined her. He glanced around the largely empty garage.

She followed his gaze. Cross-country skis, downhill skis, and a snowboard rested beside a new snow shovel. Metal storage shelves were half-filled with out-of-season decorations, several planters and baskets, and a neat pile of jigsaw puzzles waiting for long winter nights. A trash can and a recycling container sat along the wall.

"I haven't been here long enough to fill the space." Her voice echoed in the emptiness. She popped the Outback's hatch.

"Don't worry. Garages tend to accumulate stuff exponentially the longer you live in a place." Cole assessed the printer box, grabbing the handle and giving it a test lift. "If you get the door, I can carry the box."

"You got it." She hurried to the house and unlocked the back door. Max barreled out of the dining room, all love and vocal greetings.

"Hey, boy." She gave her Dalmatian an affectionate head rub. "Guess who's here." She indicated Cole, and Max pranced past Ashley to greet him too. "Inside, Max." Ashley shooed her dog into the house, then stood aside to make room for Cole.

He stepped in and paused, carrying the printer box as though it were full of feathers instead of heavy electronics. "Where do you want this?"

"In here." She led him to the guest bedroom that she used as her home office, and he set the box on the floor.

"What are you going to do with the old one?" He gestured to the broken printer sitting on a small table beside her desk.

"Put it in the garage for now, I guess. What does one do with a broken printer?"

"There's a recycling company in Glenwood Springs you might want to check out." He leaned over the old printer to unplug it. "I'll put this in the garage for you until you can dispose of it, and then I can set up the new one if you'd like."

Ashley, who had been dreading that very task, relaxed at once. "Yes please. And thank you."

"No problem." Cole lifted the old printer as if it weighed nothing. Ashley knew it wasn't heavy, but the weight and the size together would have had her feeling off-balance. As before, he didn't seem to notice he was holding anything. She hurried to open the door for him again, then followed him back out to the garage.

Max trotted after Cole, curious as ever. The Dalmatian made one of his grumbling sounds, then paused as if waiting for Cole to answer.

"Yes," Cole told him, making Ashley chuckle. "I'm carrying this printer out here because your owner asked me to."

Max grumbled again.

"It's broken," Cole explained, as if Max could understand. "It needs to go outside to make room for the new one." That seemed to satisfy the dog. When Cole put the printer down on a shelf, Max inspected it thoroughly as if making certain Cole hadn't damaged it. Then he dashed over to sniff a clump of bushes before prancing inside ahead of Cole.

Ashley took Cole's coat and hung it in the front closet with hers, then they all went to the office. Cole knelt and pulled out a penknife to open the new printer. Max watched for a little while, then suddenly raced to the front door.

"Max, you were just outside," Ashley said, but the Dalmatian treated her to an insistent protest. "Okay, okay."

She hurried over and, flicking on the outside light, opened the door. She stood aside as he darted out, expecting him to launch himself down the steps and into the yard. But Max came to a screeching halt at the edge of the porch. He stared down, peered over his shoulder at her, and yowled, his expression bewildered.

"Did you forget that snow is cold?" she teased.

He sat, yowled again, and stared down at the steps.

"What is it?" She pulled her sweater tighter and walked to the edge of the porch. Her eyes went wide. "Oh my goodness. Max, what have you found? Cole, come see!"

She heard Cole's footsteps as he hurried to the porch, no doubt expecting another catastrophe after her experiences that afternoon. However, this was anything but a disaster.

She dropped to her knees, leaned down, and picked up a basket of the cutest, cuddliest, snow-dusted kittens she'd ever seen.

4

Ashley counted as she lifted the basket. "Five."

"Does this happen often?" Cole peered over her shoulder at the kittens all curled together. They'd been napping but were now squirming, blinking sleepy little eyes as they wakened.

"You mean someone dropping off unwanted animals on my doorstep?" Ashley asked.

He nodded and ran a finger down the back of a striped kitten pushing upright with his paws pressing on the back of the gray beneath him.

"Usually people leave them at the clinic. Most don't know my personal address, so this is unusual." Ashley glanced at her faithful canine companion. "I'm glad Max heard them being dropped off. Whoever it was, they're probably not coming back."

With Max by her side, Ashley carried the basket into the house and set it on the kitchen counter. Cole closed the door behind them. Max stood up on his hind legs to investigate his find, resting his paws on the edge of the countertop. He didn't typically put his paws on the counter, but she let him get away with it this time.

Ashley lifted and examined the gray kitten. "A little girl." She set her gently back in the basket.

A patchwork kitten of rust, white, and gray stood on a black littermate and jumped out onto the counter. It must have felt strange under his feet because he stared down for a couple of seconds. His first couple of steps, he lifted his feet high. Apparently deciding he was safe, he began exploring, body slinking like a jungle cat as he sniffed a set of canisters and the coffee maker.

A pair of gray striped kittens scrambled over the side and followed their curious leader, and the solid gray girl followed.

Ashley grabbed a striped one as it went past and checked it over. "A boy."

The gray girl went right to Max, who watched the furry explorer with fascination. He'd seen kittens from a distance while at Happy Tails, but having one so near was a new experience. He leaned in to study her. The gray, not the least intimidated by his size, put out a paw and popped him on the nose.

Max jerked back, startled, and sent Ashley a confused expression.

"Give her a kiss," Ashley suggested.

Max seemed to consider this for a second or two, then dragged his tongue over the little gray's head. The kitten blinked, shook her head, then ducked under Max's chin and began to purr. He pulled his head back, trying to see her, but his chin kept getting in his way, making Cole chuckle.

"Aw, she likes you, Max," Cole said.

Max began to wag his tail.

Ashley picked up the second striped kitten. "Another boy." She put him down, and the striped pair began batting at Max's large paws.

The fifth cat, black with a white tuxedo patch on its chest, remained contentedly in the basket, snuggling down in the beautiful rich blue-and-gold brocade fabric used for a lining.

"They're going to need a litter box." Ashley lifted the adventurous patchwork kitten from the counter and set him on the floor. "Let's get the printer unloaded and use its box for litter."

Cole took the pair of striped cats in hand and set them on the floor too. "You're not going to keep them all, are you?"

Ashley shook her head. "Tempting as that is, if I kept all the animals brought to me, I'd be overrun. I'll take them to the clinic and find them good homes." She took the gray girl, who was still purring under Max's chin, and set her on the floor. Max dropped to all fours and followed the cats, sniffing and nudging them like an overprotective grandfather.

"How old are they?" Cole picked up the black one, briefly flipped it over, then held it close. It lay contentedly along his arm. "Looks like this one's a girl."

"I'd say about twelve weeks. Whoever left them waited until they could safely leave their mother." Ashley watched the bundles of fur tumble about the room and could imagine them skulking around during the night. Max would likely be unable to rest if he could hear them meowing and getting into trouble. "I think we'd all be happier if they spent the night in the garage. It's heated, so it'll feel as warm as if they were inside."

"What about food?"

"Fortunately, I've got some kitten food in my emergency bag that'll get us by until tomorrow if I mix it with tuna."

She retrieved the packages from the bag she always carried for animal emergencies and poured the food into a small bowl. Max woofed at the sound. Food was being served, and he couldn't get to it because the striped kittens were sitting on his back as he sprawled on the floor. He didn't seem to know how to dislodge them. For a hungry dog, little was worse.

"This is for the kittens, buddy," she told him as she pulled a can of tuna from the cupboard. "But don't worry. You'll get yours."

Max peered over his shoulder at the kittens climbing on him and then at her, his face wrinkled in concern.

Ashley mixed the tuna with the kibble and set the bowl aside to let the tuna's moisture soften the food a little. "Just stand slowly, Max, and they'll jump down."

The patchwork had discovered Max's water bowl and was trying to climb in. Laughing, Cole set down the black kitten and picked up the bowl. "Wouldn't you have been surprised when you got an unexpected bath?" Placing the bowl on the counter, he said, "I'll go unpack the printer. Shouldn't take long."

"Thanks, Cole." Ashley grabbed Max's food bowl and scooped a serving of his food into it. "Now it's your turn, Max."

Encouraged by hearing his name and food hitting his bowl, Max stood and the striped kittens jumped nimbly off. He galloped to Ashley's side, eyeing his food with avid interest. She led him to the spare bedroom, flicked on a light, and shut him in to eat undisturbed.

She went down the hall to check on Cole's progress with the printer. He was setting it in place on the stand when she entered the room. He gestured toward the foam packing material. "Should I put that in the garage?"

"I think we'd better put that in the spare bedroom if we're going to put the cats in the garage. I don't want to risk them chewing on it."

Cole nodded and took the foam to the spare room, where he set it on the bed. Max bounded out, his dinner long gone, and so Ashley retrieved his empty bowl and closed the door once they were all out.

Back in the kitchen, they counted kittens. One was missing. Ashley opened the door she'd just shut and found Patch trying to climb the bedspread. She scooped him up and deposited him in the great room.

Cole brought the printer box to the kitchen table. "Why don't I cut down the sides so the kittens can jump in and out? And if you're interested, I've got a couple of bags of litter in the back of my car."

"You came prepared with cat litter?" Ashley raised an eyebrow teasingly. "Did you leave me the kittens?"

Cole laughed. "I carry litter in the winter in case I need to free myself or someone else stuck in the snow. You sprinkle it under the tires for traction. Want what I've got?"

Ashley nodded. "You're a lifesaver."

In minutes, the printer box was cut to size and had a layer of litter. Once done with his task, Cole picked up the little black cat again, and she burrowed against him and began purring.

"She likes you," Ashley said with an encouraging smile.

"I like her too, but..." Cole shook his head. "Between my landlord and my erratic work schedule, I can't have an animal, even one as independent as a cat. This little one makes me wish that weren't so."

"Well if you'd like to spend a little more time with her this evening, you're welcome to stay for supper. I made vegetable soup yesterday if that sounds good. I'll add in some cheesy bread too."

Cole seemed pleased by the offer. "That would be wonderful. I haven't had homemade soup since I don't know when."

"Great. I owe you for all your help anyway."

"It's really no problem. If you'd like, I can finish setting up the printer while you prep dinner."

"Perfect," Ashley agreed. She withdrew the Dutch oven of soup from the refrigerator and set it on the stove to reheat, then topped slices of bread with cheese and put them in the toaster oven.

While the soup warmed and the cheese melted, she took the basket the kittens had arrived in and set it on the floor in front of the fireplace. None of the kittens took notice of it. Even the shy black kitty who had the good taste to favor Cole was nosing around, peeking under the furniture, leaping onto the chairs, walking along the back of the sofa. Smiling at their antics, Ashley returned to the kitchen to serve up dinner.

Shortly after the toaster oven dinged, Cole came out of the office. "Printer's all ready to go. I hooked it up to your Wi-Fi."

"Thank you so much." She swept a hand at the improvised litter box and the furry visitors, three of them now curled up on Max's pillow while he lay on the hardwood floor beside them. "For everything."

He eyed the steaming soup and golden cheese sandwiches she was plating. "This is the best thanks I can think of. It's so much better than a frozen pizza."

"I hope so," Ashley said.

Proving his enthusiasm, Cole ate two bowls of soup and two sandwiches. When he finished, he carried his dishes to the sink. I'll take the litter box to the garage before I go."

He donned his coat then grabbed the box. Max stood beside him, eager for another chance to go outside. She pushed the button that opened the garage door, and Cole and Max disappeared into the night.

She was on her knees getting ready to transfer the clan from Max's bed to their basket when they returned.

"Time to corral the herd." Cole was reaching for the all-gray girl when his phone rang. He checked the screen. "It's work. Excuse me a minute." He answered, then listened and nodded. "Be right there."

Ashley regarded him with concern. "Trouble?"

"You can say that again." Cole grimaced. "A bear has someone's cat treed and is trying to climb up after it."

"Oh no. Will you have to tranquilize and relocate the bear?"

"Probably," Cole said as he started for the door. "A bear in somebody's backyard is dangerous. Not that the bear is at fault. You build a house on the land he's lived on for years, and of course he's going to come calling. It's only a matter of time until someone gets hurt, though, usually because the human does something foolish."

Ashley joined him by the front door. "Does relocation work? Don't bears have strong homing instincts?"

"They do, and they often return unless you transport them a great distance and put some physical barrier like a lake or mountain between the old habitat and the new." Lines etched Cole's forehead. "While relocating fixes things for the humans, it isn't an instant fix for the bear. He doesn't know where his den should be or what his food supply is." He shrugged. "Life is complex."

"You can say that again," Ashley agreed.

After wishing Cole luck, Ashley stood at the front window and watched him drive off, Max at her side. The dog's presence helped fill the emptiness left by the man's departure.

"You're my good boy, aren't you, Max?" she asked as she patted his head, and he answered by leaning into her. After a few moments, she straightened. "Time to get these kitties settled."

She returned to the basket. The pretty blue-and-gold fabric lining had gotten bunched up in one corner, so she took hold of the fabric and pulled it out with the intention of rearranging it. As she tugged, a small, silver object flew out and skittered across the floor. She frowned in confusion.

What was a computer thumb drive doing in a basket full of kittens?

5

Ashley picked up the thumb drive and turned it over in her hand. Max sniffed it, and she pushed him gently back. "Not yours, Max." *Not mine either, though.*

So whose was it? Did it belong to whoever had left the kittens on her doorstep, and were they searching for it?

If so, it served them right for leaving the little ones out in the cold. If it hadn't been for Max hearing something, they could have spent the night out there in the frigid weather without food or water.

She glanced at the worn-out kittens now sleeping in Max's bed and frowned as she did a quick head count. *Hmm, only four.* A gray, a black, and two striped. Patch was exploring somewhere. She slapped the thumb drive down on the kitchen counter. It was a problem for another time. Right now she needed to track down a lost kitten.

She scanned the area, but saw no sign of the wayward calico. "Where is he, Max?"

The Dalmatian came to her side, and they searched the house. They found Patch sitting on her desk batting at the strings that controlled the window blinds.

"No, little guy!" Ashley scolded as she rushed forward. "You could get tangled up, and then you'd be in real trouble."

Patch shot her an expression of disdain at the implication that he'd put himself in danger.

"You may be cuter than me," she told him, "but I'm older. Years of experience over here."

He all but sniffed as he jumped to the floor and sauntered off to find his littermates. Whoever adopted this one was in for a very interesting life.

Ashley put all the kittens in their basket, keeping a firm hand on Patch to prevent him from jumping out on the way to the garage. Max bounded along beside her. Inside, she set the basket next to the litter box in the space where a second car would go if she had one, then flicked on the power to the garage heater. It was already tolerable, but she wanted these little guys to stay toasty warm. She hustled back into the house for a few more supplies, returning with their food dish, a bowl of water, and a fleece blanket.

After setting out food and water, she placed the fleece blanket on the floor by the basket and sat on it. She reached into the basket and took out one kitten at a time, cuddling it and talking nonsense to it. Max lay beside her, head on her knee. She was careful to hold each kitten for him to gently nudge with his nose, his version of a good-night hug, before setting it back in the basket.

She stood when even Patch was asleep. The littermates lay draped around and over each other, their natural flexibility allowing them to get into impressively complex positions. No one seemed to care about a foot or tail in their face. Smiling, she and Max left the garage through the side door.

There was about an inch of snow on the ground as they went to the house, but the stars were brilliant overhead. "Remind me to get several bags of cat litter tomorrow," she told Max. "Cole's car, my car, and the kittens all need some."

As she went to the kitchen to finish cleaning up, she saw the thumb drive she'd dropped on the counter. She picked it up. Stamped on the brushed metal side were the initials *RBI*.

Who or what was RBI? She ran quickly through the various businesses and organizations she was familiar with in Aspen Falls. No

RBI that she knew of. All RBI meant to her was the baseball phrase "runs batted in," but somehow she didn't think the little silver rectangle was storing a trove of baseball stats.

Based on the imprint's style, the drive was probably marketing swag bought in bulk by a company with those initials. Was it empty, to be given to a potential client, or did it already contain important business information? If it did, she was back at her original questions: Whose was it and how did it get in with the kittens?

Thinking its content might give her a clue about its owner, she went to the office where she opened her laptop and stuck the thumb drive in the USB port. She was immediately asked for a password. She stared at the screen, figuring it was a dead end. Thinking it was worth a shot, she typed in *RBI* and hit enter. When she got an error message, she wasn't surprised.

She pulled the silver rectangle free and put it on the desk. She'd figure out what to do with it tomorrow. In the meantime, she cozied up with Max on the sofa to watch TV before bed. It had been a long, strange day, and she was ready for it to be over. Monday would offer a fresh start—she hoped.

The next morning, Max trailed along as Ashley went to collect the kittens from the garage, where they were wide awake and exploring. When she had all five in the basket, she draped the fleece blanket over it in an effort to keep them inside. She set the litter box in the back of her car and slid the covered basket in beside it.

She and Max hopped in, and they left for work. The previous day's light snow had already blown away from the roads. Once parked in the lot behind the repurposed firehouse, she retrieved the basket, peeked under the blanket to make sure the kittens were all still inside, and, after finding the right key, let herself and Max in through the rear door of the clinic. She usually liked to enter through the main entrance in case she saw Holly, Melanie, or anyone else she knew in the lobby or the pedestrian plaza out front, but today it was better to take the shortest route.

Ellen Hayes, the Happy Tails receptionist and office manager, was in the break room when Ashley and her troupe of animals entered. Ellen abandoned the coffee she was making as soon as Ashley whisked the blanket away to reveal the kittens.

"Oh my goodness," Ellen cooed as she reached the basket. "Who are these little darlings?" She reached out to pet the gray girl, and the kitten immediately pushed her head under Ellen's hand. "What a sweetheart."

"Looks like you found your favorite already," Ashley teased.

"Hard to resist such a darling. Where did they come from?"

"Someone left them on my doorstep." Ashley smiled encouragingly at Ellen. "They need homes."

Ellen rubbed the kitten's soft cheek. "Not me, Ashley. Wyatt and Earp would have a conniption. Unfortunately."

Ashley knew she should have figured Ellen's Jack Russell terriers wouldn't be interested in a feline sister. "It was worth a try."

Max poked Ellen with his nose, and she rubbed behind his ears the way he liked. "Didn't mean to ignore you, dear."

Satisfied, Max meandered to his spot in the corner. He was content to wait, knowing Ellen always had treats for him. She gave them on her schedule, not his.

"I'm glad you're here a little early, Ashley," Ellen said. "Mrs. Katzman is in the waiting room."

Ashley groaned softly. "Really? But we don't open for another fifteen minutes."

"Since when has something as arbitrary as office hours stopped Mrs. Katzman?"

Seventy-five if she was a day, Mrs. Katzman was a big woman with a loud, commanding voice. She was opinionated, brusque, and abrupt . . . except with her dog. With Punky, she was tenderness personified.

"I need to get a cage set up for these little ones," Ashley said.

"I'll do it while you're with Mrs. Katzman, if you like."

"That would be wonderful. They'll need a real litter box and some food. I fed them kibble from my medical bag last night and it didn't upset their tummies, so let's stick with that. There should be some more in the storage room. Hopefully we won't need to feed them for long."

"Aren't you an optimist." Ellen reached out to pet the black kitten, who blinked at her with gorgeous green eyes. "You are a beauty." The kitty bumped her head against Ellen's chin, making Ellen laugh.

"You've got time to change your mind, you know," Ashley said with a wink.

With Ellen following, Ashley picked up the basket and carried it to the kennel room where overnight patients stayed. She found an empty cage and set the basket of kittens inside. They could stay here until she found homes for them. She thought they would immediately climb out to explore their new surroundings, but they seemed content to drape themselves all over each other, ready to take a nap after the ordeal of the ride to town.

"So tell me, what's Punky's concern today?" Ashley asked Ellen as she closed the cage door.

Ellen's brown eyes sparkled with mirth. "She sneezed."

Ashley shook her head, but was honestly not surprised. "Punky's the healthiest pug I've ever seen, but I'll check her over. Please put them in Exam Room 1."

Ashley went to her office briefly to remove her coat and change into a pair of light-blue scrubs with a pattern of navy paw prints. When she entered the exam room a few minutes later, Punky fairly danced on the metal examining table, delighted to see her favorite veterinarian. Mrs. Katzman, however, sat in a chair wringing her hands.

"Good morning, Mrs. Katzman," Ashley said. "And you too, Punky. What brings you in today?"

Mrs. Katzman sprang up from her seat. "Dr. Hart, I'm certain my Punky has a respiratory infection. Or perhaps severe allergies. Maybe it's a blockage. The sneeze she had . . ." The older woman shuddered. "It was unnatural."

"Let's check her out, shall we?" Ashley gave the pug a thorough examination, taking her time to be sure she didn't miss any signs of illness in the seemingly healthy dog. She explained what she was checking for at each step, knowing that attentive owners like Mrs. Katzman liked to be involved every step of the way. When she finished her exam and slung her stethoscope around her neck, Mrs. Katzman blinked at her repeatedly, worry etched on her face.

"What is it?" the woman asked. "Is she going to be okay? I can't lose her. She's too precious."

"She's as healthy as they come," Ashley reported. "Aren't you, Punky?"

Punky's curly tail waved with joy and agreement.

"But the sneezing! The wheezing! You can tell me the truth." Mrs. Katzman swallowed bravely. "I can take it."

"Punky's a pug, Mrs. Katzman. Pugs wheeze and sneeze because of their short snouts. Don't worry. She's absolutely fine. She doesn't need any treatment but your love."

Although she didn't seem entirely convinced by Ashley's glowing assessment, Mrs. Katzman gathered Punky close and left. The pug peered over her mistress's shoulder, her tongue lolling, her eyes bright.

She gave a sneeze, licked her nose, and gave Ashley a happy doggy smile as if it were a game.

"Perfectly natural, Mrs. Katzman," Ashley called after the retreating woman.

The day flew by. Dogs, cats, a ferret, a pet rooster, and a pygmy pig provided the usual variety. One of the things Ashley loved about the clinic was the diversity of patients and their owners.

Midafternoon, she escorted her last patient out of the clinic into the small lobby of the old firehouse. She knelt in front of the sweet collie who had visited today because he insisted on chewing on his left forepaw. She'd found and removed a small splinter in it. He now wore a restrictive cone around his neck to keep him from removing his bandage and licking off the antibiotic salve that would help to prevent infection while the wound healed.

She looked him in the eye. "Bart, the less you lick and chew, the sooner you'll be free of the cone."

Named after Black Bart, the outlaw, because of the black detailing in his coat, the collie pouted openly at her. He'd given up trying to wriggle out of the cone. Head drooping, he followed his owner outside.

When she walked back into the Happy Tails waiting room, Ellen was sweeping up the day's collection of animal hair from the corners. Ashley peeled off her lab coat. "I suppose I'll leave my scrubs on. I've got to make a stop at Marley Meadows on my way home to see Sweetie and her puppies."

Ellen's glance flicked to the calendar. "They're four weeks old today, aren't they?"

Ashley nodded. "I'm sure they're keeping Sweetie busy. Based on what I've seen, she's a great mom, grooming them, cleaning them, and watching over them. I doubt they're letting her get much sleep, though."

"Poor Sweetie. Being a new mother is so hard." Ellen pulled on her coat and picked up her purse. "I watch them all the time."

Ashley frowned, confused. "What do you mean?"

"Didn't you know? Garrett's livestreaming them. You can watch them 24-7."

Ashley laughed. "But all they do is sleep or nurse. Hardly exciting TV."

Ellen grinned. "Yes, but they're so cute when they do it." With a wave, she let herself out.

Wondering if she had been livestreamed on previous puppy visits, Ashley tried to decide how she felt about that possibility. Was it good PR for Happy Tails, or was she giving up another piece of her privacy? By the time she drove onto the beautiful property that housed both Marley Meadows Kennel and Marley Meadows Ranch, she still hadn't decided.

She and Max—a welcome repeat guest—went to the long, low stone-and-clapboard house with lights shining from several windows. A deep porch ran along the front of it, the kind that invited summer sitting with its white rockers. Within the past year, the addition of a new master suite, office, and sitting area had expanded the house by a third. It was Kristin's gift to her new husband, Mark Holmes.

"He moved into my house and took on my kids," Kristin had told Ashley the first time she came to the house. "The least I could do was give him a space that's his and has never been anyone else's."

When Ashley rang the bell, Kristin answered, lovely as usual in jeans and a jade-green sweater that made her hazel eyes pop. Her blonde hair fell in a wave over one eye to brush her shoulders. *Stunning* was the word Ashley would apply to Kristin, rather than merely *beautiful*.

Kristin waved her and Max in. A golden retriever named Molly and a brindle boxer named Sonny dashed over to greet them, then disappeared down the hall with Max, who was sure to return whenever Ashley called for him.

"Nice to see you, Ashley," Kristin said. As their friendship had developed, she'd stopped using the more professional "Dr. Hart" when addressing her. "Sweetie will be thrilled to see you."

"And I her." Ashley set down her medical bag to remove her coat, which Kristin hung in the hall closet.

Ashley grabbed her bag and they walked through the original living area, which had massive windows overlooking the training facilities for the horses that boarded at the ranch. In the encroaching dusk, floodlights shone on the large outdoor arena. Ashley saw a rider working with her horse while a trainer watched from a small grandstand, calling instructions. Another worker busied himself with the fence surrounding a paddock. Light also spilled from the big barn and the large indoor arena beyond. There were runs and pens beyond that, as well as a pasture stretching from the barn to the woods surrounding the groomed part of the property. It was quite an impressive spread, one that had been in Kristin's family for generations. She'd inherited it from her parents, Clint and Helen Marley.

Ashley followed Kristin down a hall toward the back of the house to a room that had been designated as the whelping room. Inside, a wooden box three feet square and two feet high had been built to provide a safe place for the puppies to be born and spend their first weeks of life protected from cold and other dangers. Sweetie lay with her back against one wall, her five puppies pushing against her as they nursed. Their little mews of delight filled the air.

Remembering the streaming video, Ashley glanced around the room. She spotted a camera set high on the wall pointing down into the box. It would capture Sweetie and the puppies as they moved around their space.

"Ah yes, Garrett's cameras," Kristin said, noticing where Ashley's gaze had gone.

"Is that the only one?" Ashley asked. If so, it was no concern. All anyone would see of her was her hands as she reached in to pick up the puppies.

Kristin pointed to a far corner. "There's another one there that captures the people interacting with the dogs. Previously we've switched it off when you're here, but I think people would like to watch what you do if you don't mind."

Ashley shrugged, making a snap decision. "I don't mind. Go ahead and leave it on."

"Thanks. Most people seem to watch the camera focused on the box. They usually don't care about the people, but I bet they'd find it interesting to see what the vet does."

When Ashley knelt beside the box, Sweetie raised her head in greeting.

"Hello, Mama. How are you doing?" Ashley reached over the side and stroked the spaniel's silky head. Sweetie closed her eyes to enjoy the scratch, then dropped it to rest on the rug lining the box.

Ashley slipped on a pair of latex gloves from her bag. One at a time, she lifted the pups, holding them firmly but gently as they wriggled in her hand. "All their eyes are open, and they all appear to be eating well." She ran a finger over a chubby little belly.

"Not a runt in the group," Kristin said with pride.

Ashley put the last puppy back in the enclosure and watched as he crawled to his mother. "They'll be really getting on their feet in no time."

Out in the hall, the back door banged open, causing both women to jump.

"Don't talk to me like that!" The voice was that of a very angry young man. "I'm not a child."

Kristin closed her eyes and sighed. She got to her feet.

"Then don't act like one," an older man replied, an edge to his voice.

Though Ashley had never met the owners of the voices, she assumed they belonged to Kristin's son, Garrett Andersen, and Mark Holmes, her new husband.

Mark continued, "Just because your car can reach 150 in six seconds or whatever it is, doesn't mean you should try it."

"Nothing happened." A taunting quality infused Garrett's voice. "In fact, I loved the speed. Can't wait to get back out there."

Kristin moved toward the door, her fingers pressed to her temples as if to hold back pain. She paused at the next thing Mark said.

"Don't you think your mother has borne enough sorrow?" The older man's voice was rough. "What if you crash during one of your stunts and get hurt? What if you wind up dead?"

"Me out of the way is just what you'd like, isn't it, Mark?" Garrett spat his stepfather's name with the utmost scorn. "You might have fooled my mother, but you haven't fooled me. You married her for her money, you greedy old gold digger. And you're going to regret it."

6

Kristin hustled into the hall. "The cameras," she hissed in warning.

"Sorry," Mark whispered, barely loud enough for Ashley to hear. "They can't see us, can they?"

"They can certainly hear you," Kristin replied.

"Like I care." Garrett didn't bother to lower his voice. As he passed the whelping room while stomping down the hall, he glared in at Ashley as if she were responsible for whatever had happened.

Ashley concentrated on the dogs, feeling awkward about witnessing such an intense family quarrel. Kristin and Mark remained in the hall, talking softly. Ashley couldn't hear their words, so hopefully neither could the cameras.

Ashley removed her gloves, tucking one inside the other, then balled them up, planning to put them in the garbage bin in the hall near the back door.

Kristin came back into the room, at her side a dark-haired man wearing a royal blue starched shirt with a logo over the heart that said *MarleyHolmes Technologies,* as though the two surnames were one. He had an arm resting at Kristin's waist.

"Ashley, I'd like you to meet my husband, Mark Holmes," Kristin said. "Mark, this is Dr. Ashley Hart, Sweetie's vet."

Mark shook her hand. "How are the pups doing? And Sweetie?" He walked to the box and knelt. He leaned over and rubbed Sweetie's head. She leaned into his touch, which told Ashley volumes about Mark.

"Sweetie is doing very well," Ashley said. "The puppies are healthy and progressing well. It won't be long before you can begin weaning them."

He gave a charming smile that appeared sincere. He rubbed Sweetie's silky ear. "You'll like that, won't you, princess?"

Ashley hoped that the charm and concern were real. She liked Kristin and considered her a friend. For her new friend's sake, she wanted to like Mark too.

"I ought to be going," Ashley said.

"Of course." Kristin moved back into the hallway, and Mark stepped aside for Ashley to precede him. She detoured a few feet toward the back door, where she dropped her bundle of waste in the trash can by the door, noting absently that it needed emptying.

Kristin walked Ashley to the front door, calling Molly and Sonny as she moved through the house. Max appeared with them. He ran to Ashley, as excited as if he hadn't seen her for days.

"I'll drop in on Friday unless I hear from you sooner, Kristin." Ashley absently rubbed Max's head. "Sound okay?"

"How about coming on Thursday instead?" Kristin pushed her hair off her forehead. "I'm having a small lunch. I've already asked Holly—she grooms all our dogs—and Bette DeVane, one of my oldest friends and Sweetie's godmother."

Ashley couldn't help but smile. "Sweetie has a godmother?"

Kristin laughed. "Ridiculous, isn't it? It wasn't my idea, though. Bette named herself to that position when we got Sweetie."

"What exactly does a dog godmother do?" Ashley asked.

"That's a good question. One thing Bette's good at is spoiling Sweetie. She also goes to dog shows with me when she's free. She was with me when Sweetie won Best in Show at one of the national meets. What a great weekend that was." Kristin smiled in reminiscence.

Sonny, the boxer, nudged Ashley, and she gave the dog a good scratch. "So lunch is a gathering of Sweetie's human best friends?"

Kristin laughed again, a welcome sound after the trouble with Garrett and Mark. "What a perfect way to put it. Can you come? I certainly hope so."

"I don't have appointments until midafternoon on Thursdays, so I can unless an emergency comes up."

"Great. See you at noon. Bette only has an hour. She's one of Mark's VPs and is one busy lady."

"I'm looking forward to it," Ashley said honestly. "Thank you for the invitation."

Kristin waited in the open front door while Ashley and Max walked down the paved path to the ranch's large parking area. Mark joined his wife, his arm about her again. He leaned over and kissed her on the temple, an easy, affectionate gesture. Kristin leaned into him. They both lifted hands in farewell, then Mark pushed the door shut.

"Well, Max, there might be trouble with Garrett, but things appear to be good between Kristin and Mark. I hope that's true." Ashley sighed, and he stared at her curiously. "Blended families," she explained. "Always a challenge."

In the lot, Ashley's Outback was flanked by two cars that hadn't been there earlier—a sleek black sports car and a silver luxury sedan. Garrett's and Mark's cars? Somehow she knew the flashy coupe didn't belong to Mark. It was likely the fast car at the heart of the men's heated argument.

On her way home, she drove past the location where she and Holly had found Edward Warner dying just a day earlier. It seemed like a bad dream now. Passing the spot brought to mind the fact that she hadn't made her official statement yet, so she made a mental note to go to the police station first thing the next morning. And, she figured, she might as well bring in the silver flash drive she'd found in the kittens' basket. For something so small, it could contain important information, so perhaps someone had filed a report about it and the police could reunite it with its owner.

After making herself a salad and sandwich for dinner, Ashley tried to watch a cute sitcom, but the accusations Garrett had hurled at Mark kept creeping into her mind. "It's the nastiness that bothers me, Max."

He lay on the couch beside her with his head on her lap. He raised his brows and blinked slowly as if considering her words. She rubbed his ears.

"You are such a good boy. I wonder if there's a man out there who would listen to me with half the interest you show." She kissed the top of his head. He wagged his tail a couple of times and laid his head back down.

She stared at the TV and gave in to her wandering thoughts. Garrett could be resentful of another man in the house, especially if he had seen himself as head of the family after his father's death. Or did the young man know something to substantiate his accusations about Mark?

One thing that intrigued Ashley was that he was not who she had pictured when Holly had told her about Garrett's online presence. Boy-band attractiveness and charm had been overshadowed by his temper at the time. The angry young man who'd stomped past the whelping room was not a cute teen with a dimple or two. At least six feet tall, he had a man's face with a strong jawline and an angular leanness. The dimples might still be there, but his fierce expression hid it.

Occasionally, Ashley would read an article about some child actor who had grown up and become old news before reaching the age of twenty. Was that Garrett? Did that have something to do with his foul disposition? Or was his anger strictly for his stepfather?

Ashley wondered if Rani shared her brother's contempt for Mark. If brother and sister stood together against a man they perceived as a threat, it must be quite a challenge for Kristin to maneuver the various personalities and emotions.

"It makes me understand why Ellen won't take the little black kitten even though they clearly liked each other." Ashley rose and walked to the refrigerator to get something to drink, dislodging Max. "Wyatt and Earp would have a fit, afraid that their place in the family was being undermined. Jealousy and resentment aren't limited to people, you know."

Max walked to her side and studied the refrigerator contents with her. She pulled out a pitcher of lemonade and poured a glass, then went to the cupboard and grabbed a bag of pretzels. She went back to the TV show, and Max wandered to his bed where he circled and curled up with a deep sigh of contentment. Ashley wished she could get herself to settle as easily.

As planned, Ashley left early the next day and drove to the police station, leaving Max at home for the morning. Police receptionist Angie Sherman sat at her desk, which was the one thing between her and anyone walking in. One of the things Ashley loved about Aspen Falls was this trust in its residents. No big city bulletproof glass or expectation of trouble. Not that this force was naive. In fact, Ashley was constantly impressed by their professionalism. Sending Edward Warner to the toxicologists in Colorado Springs was merely an example of how they did things right.

"You need to make your statement," Angie said flatly in lieu of a greeting. She was petite with mouse-brown hair, and she possessed a natural skepticism that made her both a good police station employee and one of the most analytical members of The Bookaroo Book Club she was in with Ashley, Holly, Ellen, and Melanie.

"Good morning, Angie," Ashley said. "I'm here to do just that, but I also have something for you guys. I was wondering if anybody filed a missing property report on this." She withdrew the thumb drive from her purse.

Angie studied the little silver device. "RBI?" There was a funny quality to her voice that put Ashley on alert.

"Do you know what it stands for?" Ashley asked hopefully.

Angie twisted her mouth, clearly torn about revealing information. She glanced over her shoulder as if checking for listeners, then leaned forward. "The man you found worked for Ridley Baker Investigations."

Ashley blinked in surprise. "But I found it in a basket of kittens someone left on my front step at home. How did something from his company get to my house?"

"You need to talk to the chief. He'll want your story." Angie pushed a button. "Chief, Dr. Hart's here, and has she got a surprise for you."

"Send her back," the chief's deep voice rumbled through the intercom.

"Go on." Angie pointed toward the chief's office. Ashley passed the reception desk and through a half door that led into the working part of the police station. She knocked on Chief Dan Maloney's door.

"Come in." When she did, he gestured her to the chair before his desk. "So you have a surprise for me?"

She held out her hand with the thumb drive in it, *RBI* clearly visible.

He took it, studied it a minute, then looked at her. "Where did you get this?" There was both curiosity and a hint of suspicion in his voice. Did he think she found it at the crime scene and had been holding back?

"In a basket of kittens left on my doorstep Sunday evening. I think they were left shortly after I got home."

"A basket of kittens?"

"Cole Hawke was there too, if you'd like his side of things. Well, he witnessed the kitten discovery. I found the flash drive after he left."

"Did you access it?"

"I tried. I thought maybe I could find out who it belonged to." She shook her head. "It's password protected."

The chief's smile was a bit sour. "Of course it is."

"I figured it might contain important information and its owner might contact the department to ask if it had been turned in."

"Have you ever heard of Ridley Baker Investigations?" When Ashley shook her head, he added, "They're a cybersecurity company out of Denver."

"No wonder I've never heard of them." Ashley shifted in her chair. "Cybersecurity is way outside my area of expertise or experience." She frowned in thought. "Does this drive being found here mean that someone in Aspen Falls needs RBI's services?"

"That is a very good question." Chief Maloney stood and held out his right hand. "Thank you for bringing this in, Dr. Hart. I appreciate it. Please see Angie about giving your statement. Have a good day."

With that polite dismissal, Ashley went back to Angie, who set her up with Officer Heath to make her statement. When she was finished with the interview, which was fortunately straightforward and short, she drove the few blocks to work.

Ben Sato, a friendly, athletic college student who worked part-time as a clinic assistant, met her at the door. "We have an African grey parrot in Exam Room 2."

Ashley's brows rose. "An African grey? That's fun."

"You'll love this guy." Ben's brown eyes sparkled with amusement. "He's a talker. Hundreds of words, or so his owner claims."

Ashley grinned. Typically, she saw a parakeet or canary if she saw a bird. An African grey would be a treat. "What's wrong with him?"

"I think he has an eye infection." Ben loved taking a stab at diagnosing, and he was usually right, a skill that would be a great asset when he finished his undergraduate degree and went to veterinary school.

"While I see him, would you run to Mountain Goat Coffee and get us both today's special? You can put it on my tab."

Ben's eyes lit up. "I think you just guaranteed yourself a gift on Boss Appreciation Day."

Laughing, Ashley made a quick stop at her office for a lab coat, then entered Exam Room 2. Inside was a middle-aged man with glasses and silver-shot brown curls. A gray parrot with a red tail and black curved beak rested on the man's shoulder. The bird's carrying cage sat on the chair.

Ashley held out her hand to the man. "I'm Dr. Hart."

"Emmett Yancy."

"Billy Boy," the parrot said as he bowed.

"Hello, Billy Boy." Ashley grinned at the bird.

"Hello," the bird replied.

"Be good," Emmett Yancy told him.

"I'm good," Billy Boy said. "I'm a pirate. Arrr."

Ashley laughed. Not all African greys talked, and to have one who was so loquacious was great fun. As she talked to Billy Boy, she carefully checked his left eye. There was some gunk at the corner, and it didn't open all the way. Ben's infection diagnosis was right, and she'd start Billy Boy on a course of antibiotics after she checked his overall health.

"You're a handsome fellow, Billy Boy." Ashley felt his chest and listened to his heart.

"Pretty." Billy Boy hopped onto Emmett's head and began pulling gently at his curls.

"Stop, Billy Boy." Emmett held out his hand for the bird to sit on.

"Stop," Billy Boy said. "Bad bird." He jumped to Emmett's hand. "I love you."

Emmett put him back on his shoulder. "I love you too."

"Has Billy Boy had any stress in his life lately?" Ashley asked. "Stress often sets off an infection in birds."

Emmett appeared thoughtful. "Well, we moved from our apartment to a house. That's the only thing I can think of that's different or stressful."

"Getting used to his new environment could do it." Ashley looked at the bird. "Did you move, Billy Boy?"

"Moo, cow," Billy Boy said. "Meow, cat. Baa, dog."

"Baa, sheep," Emmett corrected.

Billy Boy cackled. "Baa, dog."

Emmett shrugged and gave Ashley a lopsided smile. "Some arguments aren't worth having with him."

"I'm going to put some antibiotic salve in Billy Boy's eye." Ashley opened a drawer and brought out a brand-new tube. "He's not going to like it, but it must be done."

"I'll hold him." Emmett set Billy Boy on the exam table, then placed one hand under the bird's chest and carefully brought his other hand to his back, holding him steady. Ashley quickly reached in and squirted the salve. Billy Boy jerked his head back, but the salve hit its target. He squawked as if blindsided, which, Ashley had to admit, he had every right to feel.

"All done, Billy Boy." She held up the tube and let him see her replace its cap. "Good boy. Good bird."

Squinting his eye, Billy Boy glared at her. "Bad." He turned his back on both humans, then he promptly tried to rub the salve on Emmett's shirt.

Ashley laughed. "Billy Boy, you are one of a kind." She handed Emmett the tube of salve. "You'll need to put this in his eye twice a day."

Emmett groaned. "I'd better stock up on bandages. He's a fast learner, and he's going to go for my hand any time I get near his head. That beak is strong."

"Wrap him in a towel to contain him, tuck him under an arm, and come from behind his head," Ashley coached. "It might also help if you give him treats by doing a similar motion near his head. Good luck."

Emmett shook his head, though he seemed to be taking the responsibility good-naturedly. "I'm going to need it."

Ashley leaned toward Billy Boy. "I hope we're still friends, Billy Boy."

Billy Boy said nothing.

Emmett studied Ashley. "You're the one who found Ed Warner, aren't you?"

Ashley immediately felt uncomfortable, not sure how Emmett would know that about her. "I am."

"I was blown sideways when I heard he was dead." Emmett frowned sadly. "He was a nice guy."

"He was a friend of yours?" Ashley's heart ached, but her discomfort eased. Emmett wasn't simply someone after gossip. "I am so sorry for your loss."

Emmett became a bit squirmy. "I can't say he was a close friend. More a business associate."

"What do you do, Emmett?"

"I work in IT at MarleyHolmes Technologies."

Ashley was confused. "But Ed Warner didn't work at MarleyHolmes."

"No, he was contracted by them. Or rather, by Mark Holmes. He's the company's CEO since old Clint Marley died. Mark hired Warner to do private work."

A cybersecurity expert was doing private work for Mark Holmes? Ashley immediately wondered if Warner had found something incriminating—and if that was why he was dead.

"Billy Boy go home." The parrot bumped his head against Emmett. "Home." He walked into his cage. "Home."

"Sure, Billy Boy." Emmett closed the cage door. "Thanks, Doc."

Ashley opened the exam room's door. "We'll see you next week for a follow-up on Billy Boy's eye. Call us if it gets any worse, though."

"Will do." Emmett paused halfway out the door. "You know the funniest thing about the whole Warner situation? Chaz Romaine, the head of IT at MarleyHolmes, didn't even know about him coming. Neither did Whit Carlson, our head of security. They were both furious when they found out Mark 'went behind their backs.' You could hear Chaz and Mark discussing the situation all over the office. 'Either you trust me or you don't,' Chaz yelled. 'Take your pick.' Whit Carlson threatened to quit when he found out. 'I'm your security specialist in all areas, including cyber. Or maybe I'm not.'"

"Wow," Ashley said. "That sounds intense."

Emmett ran a hand through his curls. "You don't think either of them had anything to do with Ed's murder, do you?"

Ashley gaped after him as he left. Did Emmett just say *murder*?

7

Murder. The word banged around in Ashley's head all night and well into the next morning's patient visits. She hadn't heard anyone mention homicide, but the evidence did seem to be pointing toward foul play.

In a lull between patients Wednesday afternoon, Ashley and Ellen sat in the break room enjoying the quiet and watching the kittens tumble in every direction as they explored during a temporary release from their cage.

"No takers for these little darlings yet." Ashley wasn't surprised and yet she was. This was ranch country. Wouldn't good barn cats be in high demand?

The little gray sat in the middle of the sink and washed herself. The black lay in a sunbeam, happily toasting herself. The striped pair stalked dust motes, and Patch sat on the counter, staring upward, trying to decide if he could make the jump to the top of the refrigerator.

"It's only been a couple days since I hung the sign about them." Ellen pulled her tea bag from her mug. "Word will get around."

"I hope so." Ashley set her mug on the counter and scooped up Patch before he tried a jump he wasn't quite big enough to make. She set him on the floor to play with one of the striped kittens as it gamboled by.

"I see you have a full schedule tomorrow morning." Ellen tucked her hair behind her ear. "The Millers and the Bentleys, right?"

Ashley returned to her seat. "That's right. One of Bert Miller's cows is about to give birth. She had it rough last time, and he wants me to make sure everything seems okay this time. Then Al Bentley has a horse with a hot leg. She's an older horse, a favorite of his I've seen before. I think it's arthritis, but he doesn't like to hear that. It means age, pain, the approaching end of days. But I'll go see Darby again because she matters so much to Al. She's a sweetheart."

Ellen nodded. "I've even heard him pray for her at church, the old softie."

"That's sweet," Ashley said with a smile. "After that, I'll stop at home to get cleaned up for lunch at Marley Meadows."

Ellen grinned. "I'm glad you're getting to know Kristin. Her mother was one of my best friends."

"Was?"

Ellen's grin faded to a solemn expression. "She and Clint were killed about two years ago. A skidding truck crashed into them on an icy road. I cried for days. I loved Helen."

"I'm so sorry, Ellen."

"Life isn't always as you want." As a widow, Ellen knew what she was talking about.

Ashley sipped her tea. "Holly's invited to lunch too, and someone named Bette DeVane. We're Sweetie's support team. Bette calls herself Sweetie's godmother."

Ellen laughed. "That sounds like Bette. She's been Kristin's best friend since elementary school. Back when I was a school nurse, I used to watch the two of them whispering and playing. One wouldn't go anywhere without the other." Ellen took her mug to the sink and rinsed it out. "Though let me tell you, there was a time I thought the friendship wouldn't survive."

"I love how you know everything about everyone."

"That's what comes of living in the same town my whole life. Of course, so have Kristin and Bette, except when they went away to college."

"Did they go to the same college?"

"They did. Roomed together. Pledged the same sorority. Closer than most sisters. I have to say, Bette surprised me when she came back to Aspen Falls. You know how some people are made for the big wide world? That was Bette—or so I thought before Larkin Andersen came to town."

"Kristin's first husband?" Ashley eyed Ellen in surprise. "Bette liked him?"

"All the girls liked him. There was just something about the man. When Helen advertised for someone to work with her horses, she never expected what she got." Ellen smiled, a faraway glaze sliding over her eyes. "Picture the ideal mythic cowboy—handsome and charming, rugged and manly, chivalrous and fair—and you've got Larkin."

"Wow." Ashley sipped her now lukewarm coffee. "He sounds great."

"He was." For a few moments, the only sound was the hum of the refrigerator, then Ellen spoke again. "He'd been raised on a ranch, the third of four boys, and it was obvious that the family ranch was going to his oldest brother. Larkin came to Marley Meadows searching for his own space. He clicked with Helen and Clint right from the start."

"And Kristin too, it sounds like."

Ellen shrugged. "She was still in college when he came, so she saw him on breaks. Bette met him at the same time, and she set her cap for him the first time she saw him. She recognized a winner before Kristin did. And he was a winner, literally. He put himself through college following the rodeo circuit and winning prize money in saddle bronc riding. Had all the shiny championship buckles to prove it, not that he wore them. I know about them because my Sam read an article about him after he won big at the Calgary Stampede."

"Aspen Falls wasn't too quiet for him after all that excitement and recognition?" Ashley asked.

"He wasn't a glitzy guy. In fact, he was quiet and introspective. He loved it here. And boy, did he have a way with horses. Magic, Helen used to say. A real horse whisperer."

The front doorbell sounded, indicating someone had entered the waiting room.

"I guess break time is over," Ashley announced, disappointed that for the time being, she would hear no more about Larkin. She set her mug in the sink and glanced at the kittens, who had piled on each other to nap in a far corner, exhausted after their romp about the room. Satisfied they would be okay for a few minutes, she left the break room, closing the door behind her, and followed Ellen to the waiting room.

A little girl stood there practically vibrating with excitement. "Are there any left? Please say yes."

Ashley exchanged knowing smiles with Ellen. "Any what?" Ellen asked with restrained mirth.

"Kittens!" The little girl clasped her hands. "My mom and I saw the sign on the front door, and it said free kittens. It's my seventh birthday, and I can get one if I want." She suddenly appeared worried. "If they're still here." She took a step forward, and Ashley realized she wore a brace on one leg.

Ashley smiled at the girl. "Happy birthday. What's your name?"

"I'm Harmony. Are they still available?"

Ashley looked past Harmony at her mother and raised an eyebrow in question, and the mother nodded. Ashley relaxed. The child had passed the most important qualification—a parent who approved.

"They are. Would you like to meet them?" At the girl's almost frantic nod, Ashley indicated that Harmony and her mom should follow her to the break room. The young girl's gait was slightly clumsy, but excitement helped her compensate just fine.

Inside the room, Harmony dropped to her knees beside the pile of kittens and stared. "Oh, Mommy. Can I have them all?"

The woman's expression was a mix of amusement and horror. "No, honey. You get to pick *one*." She held out a hand to Ashley. "I'm Karen Constable."

Ashley shook her hand. "Ashley Hart."

Harmony's bright eyes remained fixed on the cats. "After I pick one, we'll go and spend my birthday money on a bed and a collar and . . ."

"We put some of her grandparents' gifts into savings and she gets some to spend," Karen explained while Harmony continued listing off supplies to no one in particular. "How she spends it is up to her. This year she picked a kitten and all the trappings."

"Last year we took some of my friends to a movie and out for pizza," Harmony said. "It was fun, but then it was over. This year my present will last forever." Her face glowed.

"You are one smart kid," Ashley said as the kittens began to wake up and stretch their legs. Patch was the first off the pile. He jumped into Harmony's lap and out again before she had time to pet him, making her laugh. Soon, he and the striped pair and the gray were leaping and romping about the room.

While Harmony watched them, the little black girl crawled into her lap and sat, leaning against her. Harmony stared into the kitten's green eyes, surprised to find her sitting quietly. She ran her hand down the kitten's back, and she began to purr. Harmony was smitten.

"Mommy, isn't she beautiful? Can I have her?"

"You're sure?" Karen pointed to the other four. "They're pretty cute too."

Harmony hugged the black close, and the kitten purred louder. "I want this one."

"You picked a cuddler. Or should I say, she picked you." Ashley thought this was a perfect choice for a little girl whose movements might be somewhat limited.

"It's a deal then," Karen said. "You now have a kitten."

Harmony's smile outshone the sun.

Ashley pulled out a paper she had prepared for a time like this and handed it to Harmony. "These are the items you need to buy for your kitten. While you shop, she can stay here where she's safe. Does that sound all right?"

"I have to leave her here?" Harmony was devastated.

"Only for a little bit," Ashley reassured her. "You're her owner now, and that means you have to do things that are right for her, not you. It's best she stays here while you shop."

Harmony took a deep breath and nodded. She held out the kitten to Ashley. "I'll be back, Ebony. I promise."

Ashley took the cat. "Ebony's a pretty name for a black cat."

"It's like the black keys on the piano."

"I'm a piano teacher," Karen said. "Ebony and ivory."

After the Constables left to go shopping, Ashley couldn't stop smiling as she put the kittens back in the kennel room and went to talk to Ellen. "That was one of the sweetest things I've ever seen."

"One cat spoken for, four to go." Ellen peeked at the day's schedule. "Ten minutes until your next appointment."

"Enough time for you to tell me the rest of the Bette, Kristin, and Larkin story. I need to know before I go tomorrow so I don't inadvertently say something wrong."

"It's in the past, but better safe than sorry," Ellen agreed. "Where were we?"

"Larkin came to work at Marley Meadows, and Bette fell for him."

"Right. So after she graduated, Bette came back home and started working at what was then called Marley Enterprises but is now MarleyHolmes Technologies. She was some sort of computer guru or something, and she did well. Clint appreciated her keen mind and made good use of her. Promotions followed over the years, so she had the success at work she didn't have in romance. She's a vice president these days."

"And still single?"

"Yep. She's watched Kristin marry two husbands while she's had none."

"But they're still friends?"

"As close as ever. When Larkin died and then when Clint and Helen died, Bette was there for Kristin. She's always been wonderful with Garrett and Rani too. They call her Aunt Bette."

"She sounds like an amazing woman," Ashley said.

"She is. You'll like her. She's a lot of fun."

"I look forward to meeting her," Ashley said as the clinic door opened and her next patient, an elderly cat with a thyroid issue, entered with her owner.

Shortly after that patient left, Harmony and her mother returned, and Ashley felt a fresh wave of joy as she helped prepare Ebony to travel with the Constables to her new home. The rest of the day flew by, as did Ashley's Thursday morning of farm visits. Once she freshened up at home and grabbed Max, she swung by the firehouse to pick up Holly since they were coming back to work after lunch. Ashley had arranged with Kristin to arrive at Marley Meadows a little while before noon so she could check on the puppies, and Holly had been eager to join.

At Marley Meadows, Kristin welcomed them with a smile and led the way to the whelping room, Max, Sonny, and Molly trailing along. The dogs peered curiously into the box.

Holly, who hadn't seen the pups before, was enchanted. She crouched and leaned over the box to pet Sweetie. "Can I pick them up?"

Kristin nodded. "The leader of the pack started walking this morning." Pride rang in her voice. "If you can call falling on his chin and lurching sideways walking."

Holly gently gathered a little ball of fur, who promptly fell asleep in her hand. She put his nose near hers. "I love that new puppy smell."

Ashley carried out her exams, each puppy once again passing with flying colors. After a few more coos and cuddles, the women headed out. As they entered the hallway, Kristin went to the back door to shoo Max, Molly, and Sonny outside to romp. The first two dogs ran along, but Sonny paused to nose at the overfilled trash can beside the door, knocking the entire can sideways.

"Sonny, leave it," Kristin commanded, scrunching her face in frustration. She ushered the dog through the door, then muttered, "Where is that boy?"

Ashley and Holly exchanged glances as they righted the garbage can and tucked a few errant pieces of trash back inside.

"Lunch will be ready soon," Kristin said, gesturing for Ashley and Holly to follow her back toward the family's living space. As they passed the stairs, she stopped and called, "Garrett, the trash!"

A muffled "Coming," was his reply.

Kristin shook her head. "I don't know what to do with him," she said, somewhat to herself. "The idea of a gap year sounded great. He wanted to earn extra money before starting college. Unfortunately, he's done little or nothing but ignore his responsibilities."

Then, as if remembering her guests, Kristin smiled with her usual brightness and indicated the living room sofa. "Have a seat while we wait for Bette."

No sooner had she spoken than the front door burst open and a striking woman, tall and slim with raven hair that had a single streak of white, burst in. She wore a red pantsuit with an elegant scarf draped around her neck.

"I'm here," the newcomer announced theatrically. "The fun can begin!"

8

Kristin had set the dining room with beautiful china, crystal, and silverware on a crisp white tablecloth. A fresh arrangement of pink roses sat in the middle of the table, their color reflected in the floral napkins.

"This is beautiful, Kristin," Ashley said. "I can't remember the last time I sat down to a table set this nicely."

"It was last Easter for me." Holly picked up her napkin and placed it in her lap. "My mom had us all over and set the table with her fanciest dishes and linens. It always makes you feel special."

Kristin's cheeks were pink with pleasure at their compliments. "Casual's great, but formal is fun every now and then."

She sat at the head of the table, while Bette was at the foot with Ashley and Holly on either side. Kristin served them quiche Lorraine and fruit with tiny croissants. Conversation was lively and fun. Ashley told them about Billy Boy and his amazing vocabulary. Holly talked about Jemima Puddle-Duck, a standard poodle, who was coming in for grooming that afternoon.

"A poodle named Jemima Puddle-Duck?" Bette leaned in, fascinated.

Holly grinned. "I don't ask. Anyway, she gets groomed twice a year—spring to cut away her winter coat and fall to trim her up for winter. A lot of dogs preen when they're groomed, like they know they're beautiful. Poor Jemima gets embarrassed. She hangs her head and won't meet anyone's eye. She slinks out like she hopes no one sees her. Her owner says she hides behind the sofa for two days, coming out only to eat and go outside."

Kristin laughed. "Dogs have personalities as different and as strong as people. That's one reason I enjoy them so much."

"Too true." Ashley savored a bite of her quiche, which was packed with savory bacon and rich cheddar. "The kittens left on my doorstep are all so different."

"You had kittens left on your doorstep?" Kristin frowned in concern.

"Sunday evening. They're cute little darlings." Ashley told the story about Harmony and Ebony. "I have four more if anybody wants one." She glanced hopefully around the table.

Everyone smiled politely, but no one took her up on her proposal.

Kristin rose and gathered empty plates, brushing away everyone's offer to help. "I'll be back with coffee and tea," she promised, then left the room.

"I understand you two have been friends forever," Ashley said to Bette.

Bette smiled. "Since kindergarten."

"What's it like living in the same town your whole life?" Holly asked. "I moved here a little over a year ago."

"It's interesting." Bette fiddled with her napkin. "You know everyone's secrets. Of course they know yours too." She raised a perfectly plucked eyebrow. "I know who used to date, who got sent to the principal's office all the time, and who cheated on their senior papers. Good for blackmail now that they're adults who project a certain image. They don't want to be found out, especially by their kids—who are probably doing the same things their parents did." She grinned mischievously, then laughed. "I often hit them up to donate to the charities I've convinced MarleyHolmes to support, so it's good to have leverage even if I'd never use it."

Kristin walked into the room with a tray holding a coffee carafe and a teapot. "As long as you don't go telling my secrets, Bette."

Bette flapped a hand dismissively. "You don't have secrets, Kristy. You are an open book."

Kristin scrunched her nose as she set the tray down beside Holly. "I suppose so. I'm not exciting enough to have skeletons in my closet."

Bette shook her head. "I'd never say you're boring. You're just not someone who keeps secrets."

"Unless it's how to raise a national champion." Holly reached for the coffee carafe and filled the floral china cup at her place setting. "How did you get started with showing dogs after being raised on a horse ranch?"

"She wanted to deal with creatures smaller than she was for a change," Bette said.

Kristin laughed. "Not too far off. Give me a minute to get dessert and I'll tell you." She disappeared into the kitchen again.

"I think it was her way of staking out her own territory," Bette said. "Sort of like her father starting Marley Enterprises."

"You've worked there your whole career, haven't you?" Holly asked.

"That's right. I loved working for Clint Marley," Bette gushed. "He was a genius. My mom tells me no one could believe it when he married Helen, Kristin's mother. She was a horsewoman through and through. He didn't even like to ride. She'd inherited this ranch from her parents, and Clint had nothing to bring to her but big ideas. They had nothing in common, but they had a great marriage."

"I assume the name changed when they were married," Holly said. "How did that come about?"

"The property was a private ranch and didn't have much of a name until Clint came along and encouraged Helen to turn it into a public business," Bette explained. "They both liked the sound of Marley Meadows."

Kristin came in balancing four dessert plates holding lemon tarts. She set down one for Ashley and moved to Holly, picking up the conversation from before. "I'm not sure why I decided to show dogs. I love horses, and I loved working with Mom and then Larkin when he came."

Bette pointed a finger at Kristin. "You did more than work with him. You married him."

Kristin grinned broadly. "I did, and he gave me two great kids."

As Kristin walked behind Holly to reach Bette, a flash of something like distress or disappointment streaked across Bette's face. But then the expression was gone—if it had ever been there—and Bette was smiling as Kristin delivered her dessert and returned to her own seat.

"I always think it's symmetry that Helen found Larkin for Kris and then Clint found Mark," Bette said as she picked up her dessert fork.

"You make it sound like arranged marriages." There was the slightest bite in Kristin's tone.

Bette laughed. "You know that's not what I meant."

Kristin nodded. "It's more like Mom found Larkin for the horses and Dad found Mark for the business."

Bette forked a bite of tart. "You're right. Your dad found Mark for the company before he even thought of him for you. He had great confidence in Mark."

Kristin sipped the coffee she'd poured herself. "He did. He used to say, 'This man is the future of Marley Enterprises.' And given what happened to Mom and Dad, it's a good thing Mark was in place as heir apparent."

"Very true." Bette glanced at her watch. "I've got a doctor's appointment I'll have to leave for in about five minutes. This has been so nice, Kris."

Kristin's brow furrowed in concern. "Are you having trouble since surgery?"

"No trouble." Bette slid up the sleeve of her jacket to reveal a large bandage on the inside of her wrist. "Carpal tunnel," she explained to Ashley and Holly. "I'm getting the stitches out today." She lowered her arm.

"Did the surgery work?" Holly asked.

"Almost pain free." Bette wiggled her fingers. "I'll probably have to get my other hand done in the not-too-distant future."

Garrett appeared from the living room, Sweetie in his arms.

Kristin raised an eyebrow at him. "Did you—?"

"I'll get to it," he said, cutting her off. "Right now, I'm giving the little mama here a break from her babies."

"Garrett, darling." Bette stood, went to him, and gave him a hug. "I was afraid I wouldn't get to see you."

He set Sweetie down. "Hey, Aunt Bette." He gave her a big smile that let Ashley see the cute kid he'd been, then he returned the hug with genuine affection. Sweetie trotted off, likely to see if the house still smelled the same as she remembered, considering how long she'd been sequestered in the whelping room.

"Want me to box up your dessert, Bette?" Kristin pointed her fork at Bette's partially eaten lemon tart.

Garrett made to follow Sweetie. "Talk to you later, Aunt Bette."

Without answering Kristin, Bette followed the young man out of the dining room. Ashley could hear the rumble of his voice outside, but couldn't make out what he was saying.

Then Bette's voice floated into the room, crystal clear. "This is your house, Garrett. Don't let him push you around."

Kristin shook her head. "Don't encourage him, Bette," she called. "He's giving us enough trouble as it is."

Bette came into the room, a smile on her face. "Growing pains with the new 'family.'" She gave the word air quotes. "That's all. Give him time. He'll be fine."

Kristin's gaze shifted toward where her son had disappeared. "Garrett's worried about his show. His numbers are still falling. That's what's really upsetting him. Mark's a convenient scapegoat."

"I told him he has to adjust his show," Bette said with the confidence of a career businesswoman. "He's too old to do that same shtick. He has to find a new format and a new audience. It's like child stars who grow out of being cute and lose their jobs."

Kristin opened her mouth to respond, but she was stopped by Garrett's frantic yelling as his footsteps thundered closer. "Mom, come quick! It's Sweetie!"

9

Sweetie lay in the hall outside the whelping room not far from the back door. She was panting heavily, her sides heaving. She shook and shuddered. Ashley fell to her knees beside her, placing her hand over the dog's heart, which was racing.

How did an animal who was perfectly fine one minute become so ill the next? Ashley checked to be sure she wasn't choking on something. No, airways were clear. Was it some delayed reaction to her pregnancy and delivery? She ran through possible causes in her mind for a few tense moments, then glanced around and locked eyes with Holly. "Holly, can you get my bag please?"

"On it." Holly raced to the front door and out. Its slam echoed across the house. Then it opened and slammed again, and Holly was back, bag in hand.

As Ashley examined Sweetie, she was aware of two things besides the dog's health. One, this dog was a national champion and therefore had great monetary value. Sure, it cost a lot to train, groom, and show her, but she earned money too. She was a brand ambassador for a gourmet dog food with a significant contract. The personable Sweetie had even walked in New York City fashion week shows, wowing the crowds and loving the attention and the applause. She added great prestige to Marley Meadows Kennel, and each of her puppies would sell for thousands of dollars as certified championship stock.

But secondly, and more importantly, Sweetie was deeply loved. However they felt about each other, the entire family doted on the little brown-and-white dog, and her loss would break many hearts into pieces.

Ashley had to get this right, and she had to make her decisions with an audience. Kristin, Garrett, Holly, and Bette stood in the hallway and watched her as she tried to determine why Sweetie was shuddering and struggling to breathe.

When she was finally convinced the dog wasn't on the brink of death, she became aware of something she should have noticed earlier. The trash bag by the back door had been knocked on its side again, and its contents had tumbled out onto the floor. Wrappers for food, balled up plastic wrap, coffee to-go cups, candy bar wrappers, even wilted flowers trailed onto the floor along with Ashley's own debris from previous visits. Of course Sweetie had investigated.

The candy wrappers seemed a logical culprit, given chocolate's toxicity to dogs. Ashley quickly discarded the idea for several reasons, though, the chief one being the immediate reaction to whatever Sweetie had eaten. Chocolate poisoning took time to evidence itself. And even if there had been some residue on the wrapper, there wouldn't have been enough to cause the symptoms she was seeing.

"What kind of flowers are those?" Ashley pointed to the stems and dead blooms on the floor. Sweetie had obviously been nosing in them. Perhaps there was something dangerous to a dog in the dead bouquet.

Kristin frowned. "They're nothing special, just flowers I picked up at the grocery store. Roses, mums, alstroemeria—things that don't die fast."

"I need to take Sweetie to the clinic where I can flush her system and hook her to an IV," Ashley told Kristin. "She can't nurse the puppies until I'm certain she won't make them ill."

Kristin, her face stricken as she watched her beloved dog struggle, nodded. "Of course. We'll take over care of the puppies."

Ashley nodded. "Make sure you keep the pups warm. Hypothermia is a danger to them without their mama since they can't regulate their body temperature yet." She ran through a mental list of the puppies' needs. "I have packets of puppy formula and bottles at the clinic. I have to come back for Max, so I'll bring them then."

"I'm sure you have work to do at the clinic this afternoon, Ashley." Bette stepped forward. "I'll follow you and bring back the formula."

"What about your doctor's appointment?" Kristin asked.

Bette brushed that away. "I'll see the doctor later. The stitches aren't going anywhere. And you have hungry puppies to feed."

Ashley stood. "Kristin, do you have a large towel or blanket I can wrap Sweetie in to transport her?"

Kristin ducked into the whelping room and came back with a blanket. As she did, the back door opened, and a pretty teenage girl walked in, book bag slung over her shoulder.

Rani—at least Ashley assumed that's who this was—froze as she noticed everyone. "What's wrong?" Then she saw Sweetie. Releasing a cry of alarm, she dropped to her knees beside the dog and leaned in to rest her forehead on Sweetie's heaving side. After a moment, Rani raised a tearstained face. "Is she going to die?"

Ashley was struck by the girl's dramatics. "I don't think so. She should be fine."

Rani jumped to her feet, face frantic. "What about the puppies? Are they okay?" She ran to the whelping room door.

"They're fine, Rani." Kristin wrapped an arm around her daughter's shoulders.

"Can Sweetie still feed them?" the girl asked.

"Not while she's sick," Kristin answered. "We'll have to do it."

Rani pointed at herself. "I'll do it."

Kristin nodded. "We'll all work together."

Rani suddenly realized she was standing in the detritus from the spilled garbage bag. "Ew!" She nudged the nearest tissue with her toe. "How did this stuff get on the floor?" No one said anything, but Rani must have drawn her own conclusions because she charged Garrett and socked him in the arm. "It's your fault! This has been sitting here for days waiting for the dogs to get into it."

Garrett flushed but didn't argue.

"You jerk." Rani turned to her mother. "I told you it was a bad idea. Gap year? Give me a break."

Garrett rubbed absently at his arm but still didn't say anything.

"Look at her." Rani pointed dramatically to Sweetie. "If she dies, it's on you."

Garrett went white. Rani again fell to her knees beside Sweetie, running her hand over the dog's silky head. Bette put a comforting hand on Garrett's back, and he smiled at her gratefully.

Kristin put her hand on Rani's shoulder. "That's enough, Rani. This isn't the time."

Rani lifted a tearstained face. "Then when is?"

"When your agitation doesn't stress Sweetie more than she already is."

Rani gazed at the dog, whose large eyes were watching her even as she struggled to pull in a breath. "Oh, Sweetie, I'm sorry. You're a good girl, and we love you. You'll be fine."

Sweetie closed her eyes in relief.

"And remember," Kristin added quietly, "the cameras are running."

Rani glanced at the camera aimed to record the people interacting with Sweetie and the pups in their box. "They don't really show the hall. And they're on mute." When no one said anything, she sprang up and rounded on Garrett again. "Aren't they?"

He became defensive. "People like to hear the puppy sounds."

"So the world heard me make a fool of myself?" Rani practically shrieked.

The back door flew open again, and Mark entered. He came to an abrupt halt when he saw all the people in the hall gathered around the ailing dog. "Sweetie?" He zeroed in on Ashley. "What's going on? Is she okay?"

"I think she will be, but we need to take her to the clinic," Ashley answered.

"Kris texted me." Mark reached for his wife's hand and she grabbed hold of him, her knuckles white with tension. "I came as quickly as I could."

"Let's get her to the car," Ashley said.

"I can carry her," Garrett offered.

Rani stepped between him and Sweetie. "Not you."

Garrett stared at his sister, clearly hurt.

"Rani." Kristin's voice was sharp. "That's enough."

Mark stepped forward. "I'll carry her." He picked Sweetie up, cuddling her close to his chest. He started down the hall, then paused. "Garrett, you know what to do."

Garrett stood with his back pressed to the wall, his face pure misery.

Rani trailed Mark down the hall to the front door and out to Ashley's car. Holly and Kristin followed. Ashley made sure her bag was packed, and as she started for the car, it was just her and Bette hurrying together across the living room and foyer.

"She will be okay, won't she?" Bette's eyes were full of concern. "That dog is so special."

"Based on what I've seen, I'm optimistic," Ashley said.

"What happened?"

"I don't know yet. That's the trouble with patients who can't tell you what they've done or experienced. It's a guessing game based on observable markers and years of training and experience."

Through the open front door, Ashley could see everyone gathered around the passenger side of the car, where Mark was passing Sweetie to Holly. A pair of ranch hands—one older and deeply tanned, the other younger and rather gangly—watched from a distance, their faces puckered with concern.

A man appeared at the corner of the house, and Ashley recognized Lowell Andersen, the ranch manager. He put a hand to his mouth and gave a loud whistle. The cowboys heard him, gave a nod, and disappeared around the back of the house. Lowell continued to the cluster of people.

Bette watched him with a guarded expression. "Ashley, have you met Lowell?"

"Yes," Ashley said. "He's who I deal with when I make a call for the ranch. He's very protective of his animals."

"He's Larkin's brother."

Surprise rippled through Ashley. "As in Kristin's late husband?" She hadn't put together the shared last name.

Bette nodded. "When Larkin got sick, he brought Lowell in to help keep the ranch working smoothly. Larkin's gone, but Lowell stayed. He's not Larkin, who was so exceptional, especially with the horses, but he's done a good job. He and Kristin make the ranch decisions together, and I thought for a while Lowell might take Larkin's place in more ways than one. But no. She picked Mark, as strange a match as her equestrienne mother and computer geek father."

"Which went well as I understand it."

Bette gave a little head bob of acknowledgment.

After Mark handed Sweetie over to Holly, he stepped back and put a comforting arm around his wife who, even as she kept her eyes on the spaniel, dropped her head to his shoulder.

"He did better with Garrett than I thought." Bette's voice had dropped to little more than a whisper as they neared the car.

"What?" Ashley hadn't followed the conversational segue.

Bette gave a slight nod toward Mark. "He didn't yell or make a scene." She glanced back toward the house where Garrett was busy gathering garbage. "But I wonder what he'll say when there's no audience."

10

Friday evening, Ashley turned onto the long driveway that led to Marley Meadows. She wished she was bringing Sweetie home. However, although the pup's symptoms had cleared up, she was going to stay at the clinic another night for observation just to be safe. Ashley didn't know for sure what Sweetie had gotten into, but it was a relief all the same to know the spaniel was on the mend.

Ashley eyed the ranch house eagerly as she approached. She was coming from the Farley farm, where she'd helped with a difficult lamb birth. She'd removed the coveralls she often wore in the field and had washed up as well as she could without a faucet, but she looked forward to the hot running water Kristin could provide. She put the Outback in park as Holly and Ellen pulled up beside her.

Ellen, who had taken Fred Farley's call, climbed from Holly's car, her face anxious. "How did it go?"

"Mama and baby are both doing fine," Ashley said.

Ellen grinned. "Good. Farley wool is some of the best produced in the state, and Fred treats his flock like they're his children."

"Must be why his product is so good," Holly put in as she joined Ellen and Ashley on the sidewalk.

While the women chatted, Ben's red Honda Civic and Cole's black Nissan Rogue came up the drive. Soon, the two men had parked and met Holly, Ellen, and Ashley on the sidewalk.

"The Happy Tails Puppy Brigade is here," Holly said cheerily.

"Strength in numbers," Ashley said, smiling at her friends.

"Everything was okay at the office when you left, Ben?"

He nodded as he shoved his hands in his parka pockets against the drop in temperature as night fell. "The kittens were down for the count, and Sweetie was settling in for a good night's sleep when I left. Jen will be checking on her overnight."

"No breathing issues?" Ashley asked, glad that the other part-time clinic assistant, Jen Lockwood, would be keeping an eye on their precious patient.

Ben shook his head. "Clear lungs, sound heartbeat, and happy tummy. She's a healthy girl who misses her family, both human and canine."

"She should be back to her babies tomorrow," Ashley said.

Ellen nudged Cole with an elbow and nodded her head toward Ashley. "The world's most devoted veterinarian slept at the clinic last night to keep an eye on Sweetie."

Cole smiled at Ashley. "Can't say I'm surprised."

"Max helped too. He's home catching up on his sleep now, though." Slightly embarrassed at the praise for doing what she considered her job, Ashley started for the house and everyone else followed.

Holly rubbed her hands together. "This is going to be so much fun."

Kristin met them at the front door, Molly and Sonny at her side. After welcoming them into the foyer, she said, "Thank you so much for your help."

"Feeding five puppies is a time-consuming job." Ashley greeted both dogs with head rubs. "We're glad to relieve you for one cycle."

"Feeding them hasn't all been on you, has it?" Ellen asked, frowning.

Kristin chuckled. "If I had to do it all alone, I'd never get any sleep. The family's been right there. And Bette too." She collected everyone's coats. "Since they need several feedings a day, we set up a rotation starting last evening. Rani helps before and after school. Mark comes home at lunch to help and does the evening and night shifts. Garrett is here for every feeding, and Bette comes before and after work."

An elegant red SUV came roaring down the drive. Bette climbed out and hurried into the house. "Reporting for duty." She surveyed the crowded foyer. "Though I don't think I'm needed."

Kristin smiled at her friend. "You are always needed. But tonight, it's merely as a dinner guest."

"Before we handle the puppies, we should all wash our hands really well," Ashley told the group.

"We can split up," Kristin said. "There's the kitchen sink, the sink in the utility room, and the sink in the powder room."

They divided up, with Bette offering to show Ashley to the powder room. "It's so nice of your staff to come help," Bette said as she led the way down the hall.

"They're not all my staff, but they're all animal lovers."

"Wherever they come from, they're appreciated. Even though there are only five puppies, it still takes forever. Turns out you can't hurry puppies any more than you can hurry a baby." Bette stopped at the powder room door and gestured for Ashley to enter, but she kept talking while Ashley washed her hands. "I can't imagine how demanding it would be to care for a large litter by hand. What if the mother died and you had to hand-feed for four or five weeks? You'd never get any sleep."

"I think Sweetie will tell you that's very true," Ashley said, scrubbing her hands with bar soap. "Ben told me she's settled for the night, probably missing her babies but enjoying the unbroken rest."

"So she is doing well?" Bette fiddled with an elegant gold pendant hung around her neck. "She's so precious to me. I don't like her being sick."

"We flushed her stomach and hooked her to an IV. Poor girl hated it, but it worked." Ashley rinsed her hands and grabbed a towel.

"I think she ingested a tiny amount of whatever made her sick. Now she's perky and wagging her tail."

But Bette didn't really seem to be listening. She glanced up and down the hall as if checking for eavesdroppers. The fiddling with the necklace continued. As her sleeve slid down her arm, Ashley could see the bandage over her healing carpal tunnel surgery site.

Bette leaned in close, through the powder room door. "Have the police been to question you?"

Ashley took a step back. "No. Why would they?"

Bette frowned. "You found him."

Ashley realized that Bette was talking about Ed Warner. "I did, but I had nothing to do with his death."

"Still, you'd think they'd talk to you. I mean, they talked to me."

"That makes sense," Ashley said. "He had business with MarleyHolmes, didn't he? I'm sure the police are talking to everyone who had anything to do with him. They're just tracing his last hours to find out what happened."

"It's so weird." Bette tapped the toe of one of her high heels. "It makes me nervous."

That surprised Ashley. Bette projected such a cool and competent image it was hard to imagine that much of anything ruffled her feathers.

"I haven't spoken to the police since I gave my official report." Ashley decided not to mention the thumb drive. The last thing the police officers would want was gossip about it floating around town and complicating the investigation.

"It must have been awful," Bette said. "Was he dead when you found him?"

Danesle see skits. Ed's last words echoed in Ashley's mind. Looking at the sharp-witted businesswoman before her, she wondered if Bette could help figure out what the indecipherable words meant.

"Danesle see skits," Ashley said aloud. "Those were his last words."

Bette's brow furrowed. "What does that mean?"

"No clue. I was wondering if you might have any idea."

Bette frowned. "Dane like from Denmark?"

Ashley shrugged. "If you figure it out, tell the police. It might help them." She gestured to the sink. "Your turn."

"Sounds like I'm off puppy duty for this round, but I ought to wash up before dinner anyway."

To Ashley's relief, Bette didn't mention Ed Warner again as she washed her hands and they walked back toward the whelping room. Instead, she talked about Kristin's family.

"Rani and Garrett have been wonderful with the puppies," Bette said proudly. "Well, you saw how much they love them, especially Garrett. And it's so sweet the way Mark tries to help. It makes Kristin happy, you know?" She shrugged. "He does try."

They reached the room, where everyone else had gathered and were chatting animatedly about the adorable puppies. While the chatter continued, Ashley studied the growing pups. Their time without their mother didn't appear to have harmed them at all, not that she had expected it to. Kristin was as responsible and involved an owner as Ashley had ever seen and had obviously been diligent in her care.

As soon as Sweetie was back and things were stable again, it would be time for the babies' first vaccinations. A few more days after that, the whelping box would be disassembled. The puppies would all be walking, their short little legs barely keeping their round tummies off the floor.

This evening, four of the babies lay in a furry heap on a heating pad set to low and covered with a fleece blanket to keep it from feeling too hot. One hungry pup was crawling around the box, searching for his mom and milk.

"Ashley, want to grab him?" Kristin picked up one of five bottles set on a table against the wall and addressed Ellen, Holly, Ben, and Cole. "I'll have Ashley demonstrate how to feed the puppies, then we'll hand out the others."

Ashley took a towel from a stack and put it over her shoulder, then reached into the box and lifted out the little wanderer, a black and tan with excellent markings. "This little guy is so cute."

"He's the one I'm going to keep." Kristin ran a finger over his head. "Molly and Sonny both seem to perk up when they sniff him."

Ashley agreed with her choice. "Pretty and spunky enough for the show ring. Championship bloodlines on both sides. Maybe another winner."

Kristin held up crossed fingers. "We'll see. Sweetie's show days are over, but I love the excitement of it all. I think I'll call him Juggernaut because he's going to take the dog world by storm. He'll be Jug for short."

Ashley took Jug and sat on the floor cross-legged, leaning her back against the side of the whelping box for support. She draped the soft towel across her lap and lay the puppy on his belly. Kristin handed her the bottle, more the size of a doll's bottle than a baby's.

Ellen, Holly, Ben, and Cole copied everything Ashley did. Cole sat with his back against the wall facing Ashley, his forehead creased in concentration. "I've never handled anything this fragile in my life, except maybe a baby bird that fell from its nest," he said. "Talk about scary."

"Relax," Kristin said with a smile. "You're doing great."

The room fell silent except for the contented little mews of the hungry puppies, now happily drinking their dinners.

The doorbell rang, and Kristin edged toward the door. "That's our pizza delivery, a bit early though." She frowned, obviously worried that the food would be cold before her guests could eat.

"I'll go fire up the oven to keep it warm while you answer the door, Kris," Bette offered. She glanced over her shoulder before leaving the whelping room. "And I'll make sure the kids don't eat it all."

"Young humans and young dogs have a lot in common," Ellen said as she adjusted her puppy's bottle.

"These puppies are incredible." Cole's face was soft with affection for the little girl in his hands as he fed her. "The animals I usually deal with are much more fearsome."

"What happened with the bear that treed the cat?" Ashley asked.

"That's a story I'd like to hear," Holly put in.

Cole chuckled. "Not much of a story. The bear had gone on its way by the time I got there. However, the cat's owner expected me to climb the tree and retrieve the cat."

Ben laughed. "Did you?"

"Fortunately, I didn't have to," Cole replied. "I suggested she shake a bag of treats. She did, and the cat came right down."

"Speaking of cats, how many kittens do you have left, Ashley?" Holly asked as she continued to feed her tricolor puppy.

Ashley uncrossed her legs and stretched them out in front of her, careful not to disrupt Jug as he continued chowing down. "Two more found a home, thanks to Ellen."

Ellen shook her head, waving off the compliment. "They had already decided to take a kitten before they came in."

"But not two," Ashley said. "That was you."

Ellen grinned. "That was me."

"They were twins, boys about seven." Ashley explained. "They won some reading contest at school last month. Their parents had promised them a prize if they did well. As the boys told the story, the parents expected them to go for the most expensive video game they could find."

Ellen laughed. "Instead, they wanted a cat."

"We let them meet the kittens in the break room," Ashley continued. "Patch took one look and tried to get to the top of the refrigerator. The little gray wandered aimlessly around the room."

"But the striped ones went right to the boys, sitting on their shoes, pawing at their ankles," Ellen said.

"And Ellen said the magic words." Ashley beamed.

Everyone turned to Ellen, who took over. "I said, 'Twins for twins!'"

Laughter filled the room, then subsided as the friends continued chatting amiably. One by one, the puppies fell asleep while feeding, their bottles emptied. Ashley placed a snoozing Jug back on the heating pad, then gestured for the others to follow suit.

"I feel a bit creaky." Ellen rubbed her lower back after setting her puppy gently beside its littermates. "I haven't sat on the floor like that since I was a school nurse reading books at circle time about the importance of brushing teeth."

"We've got hot pizza, fresh salad, and lemonade in the kitchen," Kristin said from the doorway. "Hopefully that will revive you all."

It certainly did. The kids had eaten quickly and left, but Bette, Mark, and Kristin had waited until Ashley and her friends were done with the puppies. They congregated in the large, elegant kitchen, chatting about the puppies and swapping stories about life in Aspen Falls until the pizza boxes were empty and the clock had almost struck eight.

"Thank you so much for spending your Friday night with us," Kristin said as she was guiding her guests out.

"It was fantastic." Holly's enthusiasm spoke for them all. "By the time I usually see my clients, they're full grown."

Mark went to the closet and brought everyone their coats. "It's getting chilly out there. The forecast calls for tomorrow to be another warm day, though."

"This weather is allowing the elk to stay in the high meadows later than usual," Cole said as he donned his jacket. "By now, they're typically on the move to lower pastures because the snow has gotten too deep high up. They get tired of pawing through it to find feed. So enjoy the warmth. The elk are."

Everyone stepped onto the front porch. A ribbon of in-ground lanterns spaced a few feet apart led down the path from the house to the large parking area, where tall lampposts pushed back the night. Midway down the walkway, one of the lights was out.

"I asked him to fix that," Mark muttered to Kristin.

She shook her head. "Me too."

"I'll talk to him," Mark said.

Kristin put a hand on his arm. "Be nice."

He grinned at her. "I'm always nice."

A good host, Mark led the way down the path toward the parking area and waited while everyone climbed into their cars. With a final wave, he started back toward the house. Ashley started her car, then decided to check her phone for messages. As she scrolled through a few texts, she heard a muffled cry.

Her head snapped up just in time to see Mark crumple to the ground.

11

Ashley jumped out of her car and ran up the walkway. Mark started to push himself to his feet. With a choked grunt of pain, he went back down.

Kristin reached him first, falling to her knees beside him. "Mark! Are you all right?" she asked.

Ellen, Holly, and Ben had already driven off, but Cole caught up with Ashley as she reached the couple. "What happened, Mark?" Cole asked.

"I stepped wrong on the edge of the walk and rolled my ankle." He flicked on his phone light again, and Ashley could see there was a drop-off of two to three inches between the walk and the lawn that needed to be filled and seeded. "It's my bad ankle. I hope I didn't break it."

Ashley knelt beside Mark. "May I check? I know I'm not a people doctor, but broken bones are broken bones."

"Please." He pulled up his pants leg.

Ashley examined his ankle carefully, aware that even her gentle fingers caused pain. "I can say it's not a compound fracture, but you need an X-ray to know exactly what's going on."

"I'll call 911," Bette said as she joined them, her phone in her hand.

"No!" Mark's voice was abrupt, absolute. He added more quietly, "No ambulance."

"Then I'm taking you to the medical center." Kristin was adamant. "You need that X-ray."

"This isn't an emergency," Mark insisted. "The X-ray will keep."

"A little stubborn, are we?" Bette shook her head at him.

"Get Garrett please, Bette," Kristin said. "He can help Mark inside."

"I can get myself." Mark reached toward Cole. "Give me a hand, will you?"

Cole stepped forward. "If I lift you, can you push with your good leg?"

"I'll try," Mark said.

"Let me help too." Ashley moved to Mark's side.

"On three," Cole said. "One, two, three." Cole and Ashley lifted, and Mark did his best to assist. At first, Ashley wasn't sure they would make it, but they did. Mark wobbled slightly on the good leg supporting him while his other was bent behind him, but he remained standing.

"What's going on?" Garrett appeared near the front door, backlit by the porch lights so his features were shadowed. "Aunt Bette texted that you needed me."

"Mark hurt his ankle," Kristin told him. "Can you help Cole get him into the house?"

"Uh, sure." Appearing slightly embarrassed by the task, he ambled to Mark and Ashley stepped aside.

Mark slung his arms over Cole's and Garrett's shoulders, and they staggered toward the house. Kristin followed behind, arms out as if she planned to catch her husband should he fall.

As they approached the open door, Mark grumbled, "I am not going to bed. It's too early. Put me on the living room couch."

There was a lot of shuffling, and finally Mark was lowered to the couch.

"Lie back," Cole told him. "We need to elevate your leg." He began collecting decorative pillows. Ashley grabbed a couple too.

"I still think you should go to the emergency room," Kristin said.

Mark shifted himself around, obviously in pain with the movement, until he was comfortable. "No. This is not an emergency. My life is not in jeopardy."

Kristin stared down at him, her hands on her hips. "Then I'm calling the doctor."

He met her resolute gaze with one of his own. "Call away. You'll get the answering service, and they'll say to take a couple of aspirin and come to the office in the morning."

Ashley had to admit he was probably right.

"What happened?" Garrett eyed Mark as if he thought he was faking it and was anticipating him being revealed as a fraud.

Ashley remembered his words from a few days ago as clearly as if he'd just said them. *You might have fooled my mother, but you haven't fooled me. You married her for her money, you greedy old gold digger. And you're going to regret it.*

Kristin raised her eyebrows at Garrett. "The light by the walk was never replaced."

He made a face.

"Exactly." Mark threw his arm over his eyes as if shutting out the world would diminish his pain.

Bette walked to Garrett and stood beside him. She smiled at him and patted his arm. "Not your fault," she said softly.

Garrett gave her an appreciative smile, but Ashley thought he looked more than a little bit guilty. "Is it broken?" the young man asked.

"Of course not." Mark spoke like someone used to giving orders and having them followed. Trouble was, his ankle didn't listen to authority or respect the chain of command.

"Doctor. Tomorrow. First thing." Kristin's voice was firm as she gently slipped off his shoe. "No argument, mister."

Mark winced, and Ashley wasn't sure whether it was caused by the idea of the doctor or at the pain from the movement of taking off his shoe.

Cole held out the pillows they'd collected. "Slip these under his foot. It needs to be elevated."

Kristin nodded. "I'll lift. You slide them in place."

Cole set the pillows under Mark's stockinged foot when Kristin lifted. Mark grimaced again.

His wife made a matching expression in sympathy. "Sorry. Has to be done."

Mark rested a hand on Kristin's arm. "I know. It's all right. It'll be fine."

"I know." She smiled, tenderness written across her face. She bent over and kissed him. She perched on the cushion beside him, and he reached for her hand and entwined their fingers.

Ashley glanced at Garrett to see how he handled the displays of affection between his mother and stepfather. He was watching their clasped hands, his expression a strange combination of anger and sorrow.

His angry words echoed yet again in Ashley's mind. Whether he was right about Mark or not, Kristin's new marriage was obviously a difficult adjustment for him. His father had been gone for several years, but surely Garrett still missed him and didn't want to feel as though he was being replaced.

"You ought to ice it," Cole said to Mark, breaking into Ashley's thoughts.

"There are lots of ice packs in the medical supplies in the barn," Garrett said. When everyone faced him, it seemed to dawn on the boy that they expected him to act on that knowledge. He didn't quite let out a put-upon sigh, but it hung invisible in the air as he muttered, "I'll get it," and disappeared toward the back of the house. Molly and Sonny, who had been watching events with interest, went with him.

Mark blew out a frustrated breath. "I do not have time for a broken ankle. Things are too busy at work right now." His attention went to Bette. "We have that important meeting tomorrow morning."

Bette ran a hand through her hair, barely disarranging the dramatic white streak, which fell neatly back into place. "New product being introduced," she explained to Ashley and Cole. "Last-minute, top-secret plans. Don't worry, Mark. We can have the meeting here."

"He's going to the doctor and maybe the hospital, new product or not." Kristin's chin was set at a defiant angle as she gazed at her husband.

He stared back, equally strong willed.

Bette held up both hands. "Compromise. How about making his doctor's appointment in the afternoon? In the morning, he can sprawl on the couch with ice on his foot and order us all around."

"I don't order people," Mark protested.

Bette snorted. "If you say so. But he is right about one thing, Kristin. These last-minute plans are super important. We're on a path to one-up Baldini Tech." She rubbed her hands together as though the very thought was tantalizing.

"You're the doctor, Ashley," Kristin said. "What do you think?"

Would seeing the doctor in the morning versus in the afternoon make a big difference? Since she hadn't felt any displacement in the ankle, Ashley thought a few hours one way or the other probably didn't matter. "Do you have any elastic bandages?"

"In the barn," Kristin answered. "We're always wrapping equine legs."

"Wrap Mark's ankle so it's immobilized," Ashley instructed. "If you keep it raised and iced, I don't think a few hours will matter. The doctor won't want to do anything except wrap it in a soft cast until the swelling is lessened anyway."

Garrett returned from the barn with several ice packs. Kristin took one and laid it gently on Mark's ankle. He scowled at the discomfort but said nothing.

"Put the extra packs in the kitchen freezer, will you, Garrett?" Kristin said. "Then go to the barn and get a couple of elastic wraps."

"But I was just there," the boy argued, his face becoming red with frustration.

"I know," Kristin said evenly. "We didn't know we needed the wraps then."

Based on how Garrett's fists were clenched, Ashley worried that another family fight was brewing, but Bette patted Garrett's arm and nodded to him. He took a deep breath and went back to the barn by way of the kitchen. Another crisis in this household had been averted—at least for now.

Saturday morning, Ashley found herself back at Marley Meadows. The parking area was packed with the cars of people visiting the horses they boarded at the stable. The weatherman had been right, and already the temperature was a relatively balmy fifty, perfect for practicing jumps in the ring or trotting along one of the trails branching off the ranch.

Molly and Sonny appeared as Ashley was letting Max out of the Outback, and they raced to him. Max wiggled with excitement, and Ashley flicked her hand. "Go have fun, but stay clear of the horses."

With a throaty noise that sounded like, "Will do," he raced off with the retriever and the boxer. One of the nicest benefits of moving to Aspen Falls was access to large spaces for Max to burn off all his energy, and he certainly got to do that to maximum effect at the ranch.

Ashley went to the rear hatch of the Outback and lifted the door. Sweetie rode in her soft-sided carrier, and now the little spaniel thwacked her tail against its side, her bright eyes revealing that she knew exactly where she was. "That's right. You're home, sweet girl," Ashley said as she lifted the carrier, and Sweetie answered with a little yip of joy.

Kristin met them at the door. She went down on her knees and unzipped the carrier. Sweetie shot out, and the reunion between the dog and her human was an unchoreographed dance of hugs, kisses, happy murmurs, and lots of love.

"Thanks so much for driving her home, Ashley." Kristin rose, Sweetie in her arms. "Come say hello to everyone."

"Oh, that's not necessary." Ashley's purpose in being here, aside from bringing Sweetie home, was to watch the little mama reunite with her pups to make certain all went well. Aside from Bette, Mark's business associates were unknown to Ashley, and they probably didn't care one way or another about chatting with the town veterinarian.

"Everyone wants to meet you," Kristin said. "The puppies are still sleeping last I checked. It'll only take a minute, and then we'll take Sweetie back to her babies."

Ashley gave in and followed Kristin to the living room, where several people milled around sipping coffee and finding seats. To-go cups from Mountain Goat Coffee sat on end tables and were clutched in hands. Mark sat in a chair, his foot propped on a tower of pillows topping a stool in front of him.

Kristin leaned toward Ashley and murmured, "He refuses to lie down. Says it's not CEO-like."

Ashley laughed. "It is hard to be taken seriously when you're flat on your back."

Bette hurried over, her arms outstretched. "Sweetie, you're home!"

Bette enveloped the dog in her arms, and Sweetie wiggled and whined happily while kissing Bette's chin. Even in casual jeans and a bright blue sweater with a little dog licking her face, Bette was the picture of elegance.

Kristin walked Ashley around the room, introducing her. First was the woman sitting next to Mark. "Ashley, this is Mae Peebles, Mark's administrative assistant. She's the one who really runs MarleyHolmes Tech."

"You'd better believe it," Mae said with a twinkle in her eye. She was in her fifties, and Ashley guessed that she had probably worked for Clint Marley when he was CEO.

Kristin indicated Ashley. "This is Dr. Hart, the vet who saved Sweetie's life."

Mae's eyebrows rose. "I heard. You are quite the heroine."

No, I am quite embarrassed. Ashley willed the blush in her cheeks to cool as Kristin continued introducing her to the MarleyHolmes top brass: CFO Martin Coulson, VP of Marketing Patricia Harbrook, VP of IT Chaz Romaine, and Head of Security Whit Carlson. Each time, Kristin embarrassed her with her over-the-top introduction as Sweetie's savior. Each time, Ashley managed to smile through her discomfort.

She politely shook everyone's hand until she came to Chaz Romaine. The name sparked a picture of Emmett and Billy Boy. "I met one of the men who works with you, Emmett Yancy."

Romaine, who clearly would rather be anywhere else on a Saturday morning, brightened. "Billy Boy is a riot. Emmett loves that bird."

"I do too," Ashley said, finally finding comfortable footing in this conversation. "His vocabulary is amazing."

Chaz addressed the rest of the group to explain. "Emmett has an African grey parrot who can say almost anything."

"I love it when he brings Billy Boy to work." Mae beamed. "Emmett taught him to say, 'Mae knows everything,' and he says it every time he sees me. It always makes me laugh."

"He brings the bird to work?" Mark appeared uncertain about this.

"At lunch he brings him to the cafeteria, where he performs for us. Billy Boy loves the attention, and we get a kick out of him." Mae was so delighted with the memories of Billy Boy there was no way Mark could make a negative comment. "He came yesterday, as a matter of fact."

"I'm sorry I missed that," Bette said. "I was on a call with our supplier."

"Next time he's there, let me know," Mark said amiably. "I want to hear him." He put his coffee cup down, and it was obvious the meeting was about to begin.

Kristin took Sweetie from Bette, and she and Ashley were nearly to the hallway when there was a knock on the front door, long and loud. Kristin handed Sweetie to Ashley and went to answer. She returned with a scowling man who halted at the edge of the room and glared at everyone in it. His deep-set dark eyes and heavy brows made him very intimidating—as did the angry words that served as his greeting.

"What did you people do to Ed Warner?"

12

There was a startled silence as everyone gaped at the stranger. Then Chaz Romaine surged to his feet and stalked across the room with all the grace of an angry bull.

"What did we do to *him*?" Chaz's voice shook as he got in the stranger's face. "How about what he did to *us*? I've had the police breathing down my neck for days."

"Me too." Patricia Harbrook shook her head, not seeming angry so much as amazed to find herself part of a murder investigation. "Not that I don't want to help find out what happened to that poor man, but I don't know anything."

Mark held up a hand. "Easy there, people." He fixed his attention on the newcomer. "I'm Mark Holmes. This is my home."

The belligerent stranger deflated a bit. He walked to Mark and stuck out his hand to shake. "Oliver Ridley of Ridley Baker Investigations."

RBI. Ashley eyed him with interest.

"Ed Warner worked for me." Oliver swallowed. "He was also a friend."

An awkward silence hung in the air. Even Chaz appeared chagrined at his outburst.

Mark leaned forward in his chair. "I'm sorry for your loss."

Oliver pulled in a deep breath, then blew it back out. "And I apologize for my aggressive entrance."

"You've spoken with the police?" Mark indicated Chaz's chair, available since he'd stood to stalk around the room. "Please sit so we can talk."

Chaz, who had relaxed a little, scowled anew as he realized the boss had given away his seat.

"I've been in constant touch with your police, but so far nothing," Oliver said as he sat down. "Or at least nothing they're telling me."

"Left out of what's going on, are you?" Chaz asked bitterly.

Mark sent him a stern look. "Not now, Chaz." His tone was thick with authority, the words sounding like an ultimatum.

Spurred on by anger, Chaz ignored the warning. "I'm head of IT, and Warner was investigating my department—and *me*—without my knowledge."

Mark calmly met Chaz's belligerent stare. "My private business with Ed Warner was not and is not your concern, Chaz, as I've repeatedly told you."

"Private business?" Chaz repeated hotly. "He comes into my department and I'm not told? You think I didn't research RBI? You think I don't know cybersecurity is one of their strong suits? You think I don't know Warner was investigating me? You think I'm the leak!"

Mark met Chaz's accusations without flinching. "I never said I thought you were the leak. You're jumping to conclusions."

Bette held up a hand. "If there is a leak, that is. There is no proof of that."

The others hummed agreement.

Bette shifted her gaze from Chaz to Oliver, her smile both charming and conciliatory. "How can we help you, Mr. Ridley?"

Chaz snorted under his breath as he went to the dining room and grabbed a chair. He dragged it into the living room and sat, but he was still a volcano primed to blow.

Sweetie began to squirm. Kristin sent a gracious smile around the room and said, "Excuse us. We've got a family reunion to oversee."

Relieved, Ashley nodded goodbye and followed Kristin to the puppies. Thankfully no one had mentioned her part in the Ed Warner story to Oliver Ridley. She did not want to relive the death scene with the executives of MarleyHolmes as interested listeners.

The reunion between mom and babies was immediate and enthusiastic, with the pups crowding around their mother and emitting little mewls of happiness as they did.

"Affection or hunger?" Kristin bent and gave Sweetie a last head rub before leaving the room.

Ashley laughed. "Good question. Probably both."

"Do you have a few minutes?" Kristin asked. "I thought you might like to see what Garrett and Rani do. They're filming this morning."

"I'd like that," Ashley agreed. It would likely feel like a relief after the tension in the living room.

Kristin led the way to an outbuilding that seemed small compared to the arenas and the barn. As they walked, Max, Molly, and Sonny ran up to them. They all danced with excitement, enjoying the freedom of the ranch.

Ashley gave Max a scratch while he panted blithely. "Lucky boy," she said to Kristin. "He's loving the chance to spend so much time dashing around with other dogs."

"Why don't you leave him here for the day? He did great the other day when you left with Sweetie." Kristin wrapped an arm around Sonny's neck and got a sloppy kiss of appreciation. Molly sat quietly, waiting her turn for Kristin's affection. "You can run errands, go out for lunch, whatever you want. He can play. Even when Mark and I leave for the doctor, it's not like they'll be alone. The kids'll be here as well as the ranch staff."

Ashley scanned her surroundings. People were everywhere. Owners had come to exercise their boarded horses. Western dressage students took lessons while their parents sat and talked in the day's warm sunshine. Ranch hands and instructors did their jobs. There were plenty of people to help if Max had a problem.

"What do you say, Max?" Ashley asked him. "Want to have another playdate with Molly and Sonny?"

Max's excited vocals made Kristin laugh. Ashley gave him a kiss on the nose, and then the three dogs took off once more.

Kristin continued leading Ashley toward the outbuilding. As they approached, Ashley realized the kids' studio was larger than she had thought. The outside was painted white to match the other ranch buildings, but the interior was totally unexpected. One half of the large room was open with a wooden screen blocking off a portion of the space. The other half held equipment for dog agility exercises—jumps, tunnels, walls, weave poles, an A-frame, a dog walk, and a seesaw.

The room's many lights, both overhead and on movable stands, were diffused to give a softer effect for the cameras. Two cameramen were busy filming, one with a stationary camera, one with a handheld, and a pair of monitors showed what they were capturing. A third young man, the gangly ranch hand Ashley had seen before, sat before a large soundboard.

Rani stood in front of the cameras. She wore a black knit top and black leggings with a short red sweater. "And here comes Winston Churchill, known in real life as Archibald, with his handler, Candace. Come on out, Archie."

Rani aimed her radiant smile toward the wooden screen as out waddled an English bulldog, all bowed legs and protruding lower jaw, being led by a girl of about ten. After a brief shot of both girl and dog, the cameras focused on Archie, who wore a white shirt, a vest and jacket, a bow tie, and a short-brimmed homburg hat.

"Hello, Winston." Beaming brightly, Rani knelt next to Archie and straightened his hat. She faced the camera. "Don't you love the signature bow tie?"

Ashley slapped a hand over her mouth to keep a laugh from escaping. He was Winston Churchill all right. All he was missing was the cigar.

Rani reached under Archie's tummy and undid the hook-and-loop strip that held the outfit in place. She grinned at the camera as she held the two halves out to Archie's sides. The bow tie went with the left side. Then, quick as could be, she reattached the strip and Churchill was back, bow tie under his chin.

"Easy on. Easy off." She patted Archie on his back, and he sat, tongue lolling at a jaunty angle that matched his hat.

Ashley was impressed by the ingenuity that had gone into the costume's design and wondered what kind of training Rani had, or if the girl had taught herself to sew such clever outfits.

Rani suddenly adopted her version of an upper-crust Englishman's accent. "As Winston Churchill once said, 'We shall defend our Island, whatever the cost may be, we shall fight on the beaches, we shall fight on the landing grounds, we shall fight in the fields and in the streets, we shall fight in the hills. We shall never surrender.'"

As she spoke, the cameras moved in on Archie, who suddenly decided sitting was too strenuous. He collapsed with a sigh and Rani chuckled, then she and Archie held their poses for a moment.

With another laugh, Rani stood. "Isn't he wonderful?" she asked her audience, the invisible viewers who would watch from the other side of the Internet. "Once more here are all our amazing guests." She gestured to the wooden screen, and a line of dogs and their owners emerged from behind it. "Aren't they gorgeous? And looking so fabulous in their Dog Duds!"

Ashley stared in amazement at a tiny papillon dressed as a Southern belle, a Jack Russell terrier as a beret-wearing French artist, a kilt-clad Old English sheepdog, and a Newfoundland modeling a ski ensemble complete with goggles.

"I'm Rani A., and that's *Dog Duds* for today," Rani continued brightly. "Which outfit's right for your furry friend?"

Everyone including the dogs smiled for the cameras. Kristin raised her hands over her head and clapped silently. When Rani saw her mom, her smile widened, then she played with the dogs for a few more minutes as cameras continued to roll.

"That's a wrap, as they say," Kristin said to Ashley. "When this closing segment of her and all the dogs airs, her theme music plays as credits roll, giving the contact and purchasing information as well as her website address."

"She made all those outfits?" Ashley asked. "The detail on the tiny Southern belle gown is amazing."

Kristin smiled proudly. "She does all the ones seen on the show herself. When she was little, she always made doll clothes. Her first dog outfit was a superhero cape for Molly. Then she took an old shirt of Garrett's and sewed her version of a superhero emblem on it, an M with a lightning bolt through it. Molly is so laid-back she let Rani dress her in the shirt and cape, and a designer was born. Rani was ten. She's only improved since then."

Ashley was truly impressed. "She's amazing, Kristin."

Maternal pride gleamed in Kristin's eyes. "The papillon is one of her favorite models, and the sheepdog reacts to the lights like a Hollywood diva. All of today's film will be edited down to four videos of less than two minutes each, one per dog, and one long show of about ten minutes with all the dogs. She'll post them throughout the month."

"And she'll get orders for clothes?"

"I'd guess at least a hundred, probably more. And they aren't cheap."

"How does she have time? What about school?"

"She's an honor student." Kristin grinned as Rani ran over and gave her a hug. "Great show, honey. I'm telling Dr. Hart about your business."

"How embarrassing!" But her bright smile belied the words. Rani gave a wave and returned to her guests.

"She does all the designing for Dog Duds," Kristin went on. "But as it has taken off, she has hired some local women to do the bulk of the sewing. I help her by doing payroll."

Ashley realized how she'd underestimated the scope of Rani's success. "I bet she already has a retirement account."

"Of course. That's what mothers are for. And she gets an allowance. Most of her income is in a trust, which the bank and I oversee. It used to be my dad and I, but now . . ." Kristin let the words die, then took a deep breath. "It's the same for Garrett."

The way Holly had described Garrett's social media presence, it had sounded simpler than Rani's operation. He wasn't selling a product other than himself, so Ashley doubted his finances were as complex as his sister's.

"In addition to his own brand, Garrett is also the technical guy behind all this." Kristin waved her hand around the room. "He designed the studio. The cameramen are high school friends of his who are planning on careers in film. The sound guy is his friend Henry." She pointed to the glass-fronted sound booth.

"That's great that the kids brought in their buddies," Ashley said.

"At first, his friends got involved for the fun of it, just like Garrett and Rani. But when the kids started making money, it was only fair to pay the guys too. Garrett meets with them before each taping to go over everything, then Garrett and Henry do all the technical work of putting the shows together. The boys know their way around some serious software."

It took a few minutes for Rani and her models to leave the set and for the cameramen to set up for Garrett's agility program. During that time, Kristin fussed over each of the dogs and introduced Ashley as Dr. Ashley Hart, Aspen Falls's new vet, to all the owners. "She saved Sweetie's life the other day," she told them. "You want to get to know her."

Ashley tried to smile even as she felt her face go scarlet at the repeated praise.

When Archie and the others were being led out of the building, Sonny came charging in, followed by Molly and Max. Sonny went right to the agility course and began running it. He leaped over the jumps with speed and grace. Max watched for a few jumps, then he followed suit, clearing the hurdles with ease.

"He's a natural," Kristin said.

"Maybe I'll get him into agility training," Ashley said, equally impressed at Max's hidden talent.

Sonny cleared another jump and ran into one of the tunnels. Max took the jump and followed Sonny to the beginning of the tunnel, but stopped so quickly he almost sat down. Sonny popped out the far end and headed for the A-frame. Max decided to ignore the tunnel, instead chasing the boxer up the A-frame.

Sonny raced down and on to the next challenge. Max teetered at the top. The Dalmatian hadn't foreseen going down at such a severe angle. He took a hesitant step down, then another. Clearly unhappy with his location, he huffed in annoyance and took a great leap to the ground. Ashley's breath caught as she watched him land on his long, fragile legs.

Molly, who hadn't done a single agility trick, raced to Max as if to make sure he was all right.

"Mom!" Garrett shouted from across the room.

"Yes, Garrett. I know." Kristin clapped her hands. "Sonny, Molly, Max, come on. Time to go."

Ashley watched Max as he raced to Kristin with the others. He was as agile as always, so he must not have suffered any negative effects from his daring leap. Kristin ushered the dogs to the door and sent them out, closing the door behind them.

Garrett stormed over, thunderclouds in his expression. "What were they doing in here?"

"You know Sonny loves agility," Kristin said.

"Any day but a filming day when it's off-limits to him and Molly," Garrett snapped. With an annoyed glare at Ashley, he added, "And everyone else."

Kristin put a hand on his arm. "Easy there."

"It was Rani, wasn't it?" Garrett growled. "She let them in on purpose to bug me. I should quit on her. Then she'd show me a little respect."

Kristin fixed a steely gaze on her son. "Garrett, I'm going to assume your bad attitude is because you're nervous about the new format for your show. I'm going to assume you don't mean to be impolite to our guest or to me. I'm going to suggest you calm down because I think everyone's ready for you."

Garrett cast a glance at the cameramen and sound guy, who were watching and listening. His anger drained away, replaced by something resembling embarrassment. He took a deep breath and mumbled, "Sorry," then strode to where a woman and her German shepherd waited for him.

Kristin watched him go. "Sometimes he doesn't handle the stress well. The last two years have seen a consistent decline in followers, advertising, and revenue."

Ashley nodded, recognizing the words as both an explanation and an apology. She studied Garrett, now appearing quite affable as he spoke with his guest. What was it like to be such a success and then to see it fade away, at least in your own eyes, all before your twentieth birthday?

"Ok, ready," Garrett called. The cameramen trained their lenses on him, and he gave a winning smile. "Hey, dog lovers," he said brightly, all charm and good looks.

Ashley saw tears gather in Kristin's eyes as she watched her son. Despite Garrett's sunny on-air personality, a gathering storm continued to threaten his family. When the storm broke, would it destroy everything this young man held dear?

13

As though Garrett had flipped a switch, he shot the camera a winning smile while he introduced his guests. "This handsome German shepherd is Percy, and he's brought his human, Cheri, with him. I'm going to be instructing them—and you—on the finer points of agility training. First, though, Percy is going to run the course to show us his stuff." He gave Percy a nod. "Good luck."

Cheri and Percy went to the beginning of the course. Percy crouched, ears pricked, waiting for the signal to go.

"Okay, Cheri," Garrett said.

Cheri gave the signal, and Percy took off, sailing over the first jumps. Cheri ran beside him, instructing him as he leaped and climbed and tunneled. The cameras followed the dog's progress from different angles.

At the end of the run, Percy pranced with pride. "Way to go, Percy!" Cheri cheered as she gave him a treat.

"Well done," Garrett said to both owner and dog as he gave Percy a treat too, then he turned to the camera. "You'll notice Percy did well on the tunnel and all the jumps. He had great height and speed. He did, however, have some trouble on the contact equipment like the seesaw and A-frame. In his excitement, he didn't touch the contact zone at the end of each piece, which is required. You'll notice the contact zone is a different color than the rest of the equipment. We have to teach Percy to slow down as he exits the pieces so he touches the contact zone, or he'll be disqualified in competition."

As Garrett spoke, Percy glanced from Garrett to Cheri, anxious for the fun of running the course again.

Still addressing the camera, Garrett said, "Percy loves the speed of the course. You can tell by watching his legs stretch as he eats up space. This is both good and bad. We're going to try it once more, slowing Percy as needed to teach him about those key contact spots."

Ashley watched Percy with a keen eye. Having attended agility competitions, she knew how amazing dogs could be on the course. And they loved it. They quivered with anticipation before they got the go signal, and when they finished, they jumped with joy and accomplishment. The trick would be to train Percy to hit those contact spots without killing his speed and his delight.

Kristin touched Ashley on the arm and indicated they should head out. They left as quietly as they'd entered. Kristin smiled serenely, all signs of concern for her son gone.

"That was wonderful, Kristin," Ashley said once they were outside. "Thanks for letting me watch. Your kids are amazing."

Kristin beamed. "I'm so proud of them. After Larkin died, they were so lost, so sad. I tried to help, but my grief was eating at me too. My dad got them making home movies with an old video camera, then with their cell phones, and now with professional equipment. They each developed their specialty."

"It's easy to see Rani's talent with sewing, and she sparkles on screen. Garrett seems very comfortable in front of the cameras as well."

"He is, but he used to sparkle too," Kristin said. "When he was a young teen, he played with puppies and beamed for all the young girls who thought he was adorable. Then he matured physically, and he's trying to figure out how his show can grow as he has." She flicked her hand toward the studio. "This agility thing is his latest attempt to find a new sweet spot." She pursed her lips. "I won't tell him unless he asks, but I don't think this is it."

"Too many other shows about the same thing?"

Kristin nodded. "People who are winning national competitions are putting up videos all the time. Why should people follow Garrett, who doesn't train professionally, when they could watch someone who trains champions?"

Ashley hesitated, then asked, "Has he considered stepping back from being an online personality?"

"It's what he knows. This gap year is supposed to give him the opportunity to discover his new path. He used to be so cute just rolling around in the grass with the dogs and puppies that young girls flocked to his site. He also added real knowledge about breeds and caring for your dog. But now? He's grown up, and so has his audience. It's all disappeared."

"Aging out at eighteen or nineteen has to be so hard."

"He thinks he needs to continue to make money." Kristin paused beside the training arena fence and watched as a teen girl rode her horse through a series of obstacles. "His little sister is beating him more each day. His various attempts at a new format aren't attracting audiences or advertisers, while Rani effortlessly pulls in followers, advertisers, and money. Making money is nice at any age, but earning it as a teen makes you feel that's your value as a person. And when it no longer comes, there goes your identity and self-worth. Young people always struggle to figure out who they are, but it's worse when you used to be successful at something that doesn't work for you anymore."

Lowell Andersen came out of the barn and saw them. He waved, and they waved back.

"Has Lowell mentioned how Saffron's hoof is doing?" Ashley asked. "The infection should have cleared up, but maybe I ought to check on him while I'm here."

"Lowell told me it seems to be healing, but you're welcome to go visit him while you're here if you have time." Kristin checked her watch. "I ought to get back to the house and start moving Mark in the direction of that doctor's visit."

"Good luck," Ashley said, then walked over and met Lowell between the barn and the pasture. "How's Saffron doing?"

"He seems right as rain thanks to that salve you gave us," Lowell said. "Come see for yourself."

They strolled toward the pasture fence, beyond which three horses were grazing. Lowell leaned against the rail, and Saffron, a chestnut gelding whom Ashley had recently treated for a hoof infection, came to the fence and nosed at the ranch hand. Lowell laughed and pulled a carrot from his pocket. Spotting treats being handed out, the other two horses were beside Saffron in a flash.

"We're getting a new mare tomorrow," Lowell said to Ashley while he handed carrots to each horse. "I think she's going to be a problem. I would have refused her for the sake of the other horses, but you know Kristin. She wants to give Skye a chance."

"Anything I can do?" Ashley asked.

"We might need tranquilizers. Maybe pain meds. Her new owner is having trouble with her. She's either lethargic or aggressive. The vet who's dealt with her previously says she's healthy, but something's not right. Didn't say what, though." He heaved a resigned sigh. "She sounds like more trouble than she's worth if you ask me."

"Lowell, that surprises me. You're usually such a softie when it comes to horses."

He shrugged. "From what I hear, I'm thinking they should find her a nice farm and let her out to pasture for the rest of her life. But her owner wants to keep her for riding. The hope is that our care and attention will solve whatever's bothering her."

"It's worth trying," Ashley said. "I'll send over the meds, then I'll stop in tomorrow afternoon to check on her."

"Sounds good." Lowell walked to the gate. "Now that Saffron has had his dessert first, want to see how that hoof is healing?"

Saffron's hoof did appear to be almost back to normal, to Ashley's relief. After she checked him over, she went with Lowell into the barn and greeted the other horses. Lowell introduced her to several owners as the ranch's vet, and she enjoyed talking everything equestrian with people who obviously loved horses. After a pleasant visit, she bid Lowell goodbye and wandered toward her car.

She stopped as she rounded the house. The gangly ranch hand she'd seen in the sound booth was by the path from the house, a wheelbarrow of soil and a shovel beside him. He was filling in the drop along the walkway.

Wasn't that Garrett's responsibility? Had he somehow conned this guy into doing his job?

She walked to the boy. "How's it going?"

He glanced up, surprised someone was talking to him. Dirt dribbled from the end of the shovel in his hand. "Just another job to keep Marley Meadows at the top of the heap."

What was that emotion she was hearing? Resignation? Resentment? Or was it a plain old comment with no hidden meaning?

"I'm Ashley Hart, the veterinarian." She held out her hand.

He blinked, brushed his against his worn jeans, then offered it. "I'm Henry."

"Nice to meet you." She assessed Henry's work. "Can I offer some advice?"

"Okay."

"You ought to tamp down that soil and add more. Otherwise, it will compact on its own and you'll still have a drop-off, just not as big."

"Oh." Henry studied the dirt he'd distributed as if he hadn't the vaguest idea what tamping meant.

"Get on your knees and press down with your hands." She pushed on the air in front of her.

He shrugged and obeyed. He looked up in surprise when the soil sank. "Thanks. No one ever tells me anything."

"Have you worked here long?"

"Sorta. I know Garrett."

"He's a good friend?" *Or someone who uses you to do his dirty work?*

"You know Garrett." The corner of Henry's mouth quirked. "He's . . . Garrett, you know?"

As if summoned, Garrett appeared from the house and started toward Henry. Ashley decided it was time to move along, so she gave Henry a wave, directed one at Garrett as he neared, and walked on. When she reached the Outback, she paused to watch but tried not to be too obvious. For some reason, she felt nervous for Henry.

When Garrett reached Henry, they started talking, but Ashley noticed Garrett didn't offer to help. Instead, he only had criticism for his friend.

"Geez, Henry." Garrett's frustrated comment carried clearly, but none of what followed was audible.

Henry reared back on his knees, hands wide, as he talked to Garrett. Garrett merely shook his head at whatever Henry was saying.

The house front door opened, and Bette exited. When she reached Garrett and Henry, she stopped and spoke to them briefly. Garrett said something that made her laugh. Henry, still on his knees, laughed too and made a comment.

Bette continued on her way. When she saw Ashley, she veered in her direction. "All the MarleyHolmes folks have gone home," she announced. "So has Mr. Ridley. Kristin and Mark are facing off over the doctor's visit. The idiot man doesn't want to go." She gave a puff of laughter. "However, I'd bet on Kristin if I were a gambling woman."

"She's certainly got a way about her," Ashley agreed. "She took me to watch the kids recording their shows."

"Fascinating, isn't it?"

"Very impressive. Then I talked with Lowell for a while." She checked her watch, surprised to see it was well after lunchtime. Her tummy rumbled. "Now I need lunch."

"Me too. Want to join me at Miss Abigale's Tea Room if she has an opening?"

Ashley smiled, eager for a chance to have lunch with a new friend. "That sounds lovely."

"Let me call and check." Bette did and gave Ashley a big grin as she said into her phone, "We'll be there soon, Abigale." She hung up. "She says she can seat us anytime."

Ashley glanced down at her outfit and noticed she'd gotten dirt smeared across the hem of her jeans while she'd been with the horses. "Do you mind if I stop at home and change first? I can meet you at the tearoom."

"I'll come with you," Bette said. "I'd love to see your house."

Ashley hesitated, wondering if she'd left things neat enough for company. Deciding she had, she agreed, and soon they were on their way, each driving her own car. Once at the house, Ashley welcomed Bette inside and gave her a brief tour.

"This is so cute," Bette said as they stood in the hallway and peeked their heads into the spare bedroom. "The neutrals are all very calming."

"Thanks." Ashley gestured to the office door. "This one is my office, but I haven't done much with the decor yet."

Bette clasped her hands. "Oh, I love to give decorating advice." She made a shooing motion. "Why don't you go change and I'll scope out what you're working with."

Having admired Bette's style since meeting her, Ashley readily agreed. After she slid into fresh jeans and her favorite fall sweater, she joined Bette in the office, and they spent a few minutes discussing furniture placement and wall colors. Ashley's stomach grumbled again, and they left for Miss Abigale's.

Once they were seated at the restaurant and had ordered, Bette eyed Ashley. "What did you think of Oliver Ridley?"

Ashley considered. "Strong personality. Intimidating appearance with those dark, heavy brows. Genuinely upset over Ed Warner. Used to getting his way. Super intelligent."

Bette appeared impressed. "You could tell all that?"

"Well, maybe not the intelligent part. I'm assuming that considering what his company does."

"Cybersecurity."

A server placed avocado toast in front of Bette and a cup of tomato bisque in front of Ashley. With a flourish, he poured hot tea from each woman's individual teapot into her floral china cup, then moved on.

Bette took a sip of tea and winced. "Piping hot." She set the cup down. "You haven't heard anything more, have you?"

Ashley blew on her own tea to cool it. "Anything more about what?"

"About Ed Warner and why he was at MarleyHolmes."

Ashley felt a zap of surprise. "Why would I know anything about that?"

"I don't know. 'Danesle see skits' maybe? I keep running that phrase through my mind, trying to figure out what it means."

"Any ideas?" Ashley took a quick sip of her hot tea, then set the cup down and took up her soup spoon.

Bette shook her head and vaguely waved a perfectly manicured hand. "I find myself feeling a bit lost. Clint Marley would never have brought in someone to spy on us. And I'm not the only one who's upset. You heard Chaz. And Patricia. Even Martin, the finance guy and ultimate team player, is unhappy. Whit, the head of security, probably has teeth marks in his tongue from biting it in his effort to keep from speaking his mind."

Ashley frowned as she stirred her soup. She understood the anger and upset. Hiring someone like Ed Warner secretly seemed to indicate Mark didn't trust one of his upper-echelon team members. Was he concerned about business espionage? If Ed hadn't died, would anyone at MarleyHolmes have known about him and his investigation?

But what if he'd lived long enough to find something? If he'd identified the leak, why hadn't he told Mark?

Or had he?

Bette leaned forward, arms resting on the table, as if she was imparting privileged information. "I can't tell Kristin this, but I wonder about Mark's ability to lead a firm like ours."

Ashley wanted to pull away, to put distance between herself and that statement. *Stop, Bette. Not my business.*

Bette smiled at her. "It's nice to have someone I can talk to about it. Friends you can trust are all too rare."

Ashley took a bite of soup. Friends were one thing. Confidants were another. That position was earned over time. Somehow this conversation with someone she barely knew felt unprofessional, unkind, and unfair to Kristin.

Their server returned with trays of savory tea sandwiches, sweet cakes, and scones with lemon curd and clotted cream on the side.

"This looks amazing." Ashley smiled at Bette, thinking it was the perfect time to change the direction of this conversation. "Do you eat here often?"

But Bette wasn't deterred. "I do." She picked up a scone and broke it open. "I hope Mark isn't somehow bleeding the company dry, either through unnecessary expenses like hiring Ed Warner or through plain old mismanagement. When Clint first hired him, I thought he was a good addition. Now . . ."

Ashley glanced at Bette, hoping she was going to stop discussing MarleyHolmes business with her.

But the other woman didn't meet Ashley's gaze. Instead, she focused on layering lemon curd and clotted cream on half of a scone as she spoke. "It would be terrible if the company folded under his leadership. We have such a good name in our industry, and I'm proud to say I helped build it. So if anything goes wrong, my reputation is on the line." She hummed with pleasure as she took a bite. "If we go under, it won't do my bank account any good either."

Ashley picked up a tea sandwich of roasted turkey and cranberry chutney. She didn't know what to say. Was MarleyHolmes really in trouble, or was Bette worrying over nothing? If the business collapsed, it would be another blow to Kristin and a blot on Mark's resume, to say nothing of the job losses for so many people, including Bette.

But why would Bette talk to Ashley about it? She wasn't part of the problem or part of the solution. She took a bite of her sandwich. "This is delicious," she said after she'd washed it down with some tea.

Bette smiled, her red lipstick still perfect despite eating and drinking. "I love the variety of flavors in a tea tray like this, don't you?"

"I do." With relief, Ashley followed the conversation to favorite foods, then Bette's recommendations for the best shopping in town and the nearby area.

"Have you been to Eagle's Nest Gifts? It's just down the street. Let's go over and I'll introduce you to the owner, Marylouise Decker.

You'll like her. She's from back East somewhere. Maybe you know some of the same people."

Ashley bit back a grin at Bette's amusing generalization.

Eagle's Nest Gifts was a lovely little shop. Marylouise, who had never been to Ohio, let alone Ashley's hometown of Dayton, had great variety and exquisite taste. No cheap tchotchkes here. Instead, stylish embroidered sweatshirts and screen-printed tees were neatly folded and stacked in cubbies, turquoise jewelry and silky scarves filled display cases, high-quality cowboy hats topped a carved wood rack, and beautiful framed Colorado photography lined the walls.

A lovely collection of Navajo pottery caught Ashley's eye. Bowls, bottles, narrow-necked vases, and whimsical animal figures sat on a shelf, the traditional geometric patterns bringing life to the beautiful shapes. An aqua turtle with an exaggeratedly domed shell particularly appealed to her. She'd read that, in Navajo culture, the turtle symbolized creation, good health, and long life.

Ashley picked it up, turned it over, and saw two things that surprised her. One was the signature of the artist, Margaret White Bear. The other was the price tag. Given it was a one-of-a-kind piece, she'd expected it to be much more expensive. How could she resist something so perfect?

Before she talked herself out of it, she went to the checkout counter, where a high school girl was waiting on a woman with her arms full of Western souvenirs. Gifts for everyone back home, Ashley guessed. This woman alone would make it a good day for Eagle's Nest Gifts.

While she waited in line, Ashley saw Bette talking with Marylouise over by a clothing rack topped with a sign that read *Local Wool Sweaters*. Ashley wondered if they were made with Farley wool. She took a step in that direction, then caught herself. She didn't really have time to browse, so she stayed in line, telling herself she'd come back another day to admire the sweaters.

The sun would soon be slipping behind the mountains, and she needed to pick up Max. As she tried to catch Bette's eye to let her know she'd be leaving shortly, Marylouise handed Bette a piece of paper. Bette read it and nodded.

As they walked toward the cash register, Ashley heard Bette say, "I'm glad you're doing so well with them. Margaret will be so pleased about the new order."

Marylouise grinned happily. "They're selling like crazy. Thanks for connecting us."

Ashley flipped her turtle over. Was Margaret White Bear a friend of Bette's? How interesting it must be to know someone so creative.

Ashley was paying for her purchase when Bette reached her. "I've got another appointment, Ashley. Thanks for having lunch with me."

Bette was gone before Ashley had the opportunity to ask about knowing Margaret White Bear, so she figured she'd bring it up another time. She carried her new treasure to the Outback with a smile.

A short time later, Ashley parked in the Marley Meadows lot. She was wondering how she'd ever find Max on this expansive spread when Kristin and Mark pulled in beside her in their luxury sedan. Kristin climbed out of the car and hurried around to the passenger side. She opened the back door and pulled out a pair of crutches. Mark used the doorframe as leverage to get himself to his feet, then took the crutches and slid them under his arms. He began a slow walk to the house while Kristin followed.

"How did it go?" Ashley asked as she caught up to Kristin on the sidewalk. "I see they sent you home."

"Only until I have surgery at the hospital in Vail on Monday for my torn ligament." Mark paused to study the soil that now filled the dangerous little drop-off by the walk, then he glanced back at Kristin. "He did it."

"Told you he would." Kristin wrapped her scarf more snugly around her neck.

Mark grinned at her. "How you love to be right."

"I do." Kristin's expression was smug, but her eyes twinkled.

"Maybe there's hope for him yet," Mark said.

Ashley bit her lip. If they knew Garrett had merely watched, they'd be so disappointed. Instead of mentioning what she'd seen, she asked, "How do you get the dogs to come when they've been roaming all day?"

"With this." Kristin reached into her coat pocket and pulled out a dog whistle.

Mark chuckled. "She's got those all over the place."

Kristin put the whistle to her lips and blew. "They know they get fed if they respond."

A tornado of fur raced onto the front porch. Molly and Sonny sat expectantly. Max, who had no idea what was going on, leaned into Ashley for a good scratch. His tongue was lolling, and his eyes were bright. He'd had a great day.

"Since he doesn't know about the f-o-o-d, I'll take him home. Thanks for letting him have fun with Molly and Sonny."

"Anytime," Kristin said with a smile. "They love him."

After exchanging goodbyes, Ashley withdrew Max's leash from her pocket, clipped it on, and led him to the car.

When they reached home, Max collapsed on his bed and was asleep before Ashley had her coat hung up. She took the little gift bag from Eagle's Nest Gifts and unwrapped her turtle. She set it on the coffee table and grinned. The lovely turquoise brightened the room.

She wasn't that hungry after her late lunch, so she grabbed a premade smoothie from the refrigerator and sat in front of the TV.

She'd taken one sip when a noise set her hair on end.

14

"What in the world?" Ashley pushed to her feet and, setting her drink aside, hurried toward the office, the source of the sound. Exhausted, Max didn't even twitch at the strange noise.

She stopped in the office doorway and stared. Page after page of coded gibberish—at least that's what it was to her—poured from her new printer. She hadn't paid much attention to Cole's test printing the other day, so she hadn't recognized its mechanical swishing and whirring. Some of the freshly printed sheets rested in the paper holder, while others had overshot the device and covered the floor. She began picking them up, scanning them as she did. Line after line of letters and symbols filled the sheets.

She grabbed her phone and called Cole.

"Hey," he said, his warm tone already making her feel calmer.

"Hi," she replied. "Are you on duty at the ranger station?"

"Yeah, but I have a few minutes. What's up?"

She bit her lip, knowing how this would sound. Best to get it over with. My printer's printing, but I didn't ask it to."

"What do you mean?"

"I was sitting in the other room when it began printing all on its own. It must have printed at least thirty pages already."

"And it's not a document you printed?"

"I just got home and I haven't touched my computer all day."

"What is it?" He chuckled. "The first draft of someone's novel?"

"Very funny," she answered. "It's some kind of code. How do I stop it?"

"There should be a cancel button. If you can't find it, check the manual."

She scanned the face of the printer but didn't see an obvious cancel button. "Where's this coming from?" she asked as it continued to print.

"Is your Wi-Fi network secure? Maybe somebody nearby accidentally sent a file to your printer."

Just as Ashley was about to root around for the manual, a final sheet flew out that was surprisingly readable. Ashley grabbed it. "Okay, this is a mailing label," she reported. "And now it's stopped printing."

"What does the label say?"

"It's addressed to Baldini Technologies in Gypsum, Colorado. Where's Gypsum?"

"A little northwest of us."

"What does Baldini Technologies do? It sounds familiar."

"No idea. Is there a return address on the label?"

Ashley scanned the page again. "William Cody in a town named Aladdin."

Cole was laughing again. "William Cody? As in Buffalo Bill?"

"Hawke?" A sharp voice distorted by radio transmission carried across the phone line. "Just got a call about some high school kids planning a bonfire off the Jasper Pines Trail."

"Roger that," Cole answered. "Sorry, Ashley, I've got to go break this up before we have a forest fire. See you Monday night."

When he hung up, Ashley scoffed. How could those teens not recognize the danger of having a bonfire in the middle of the dry season?

And what did Cole mean about Monday night?

She stacked all the computer code pages and placed the Baldini Technologies label on the bottom. She slid them into a folder and put them on her desk. Maybe she'd ask Bette's advice about what to do with them since she had spent years working with computers before moving up to management. Bette seemed like the kind of person who always knew what to do.

Ashley wandered back to the living room, where Max slept on. She'd barely taken a seat when her cell rang. "Are you busy Monday night?" Holly asked.

"No," Ashley answered, starting to put things together.

"Good. You're my second call."

"And Cole was your first."

There was a surprised pause. "How'd you know that?"

"I just got off the phone with him. He said he'd see me Monday, but before he could explain what that meant, he had to go break up a bonfire in the forest."

"You can't have fires right now," Holly said. "It's posted everywhere. Things are dry as tinder."

"Tell that to those high school students."

"Well Cole will definitely earn his dinner dealing with that," Holly said. "Ryan won a door prize at some work function—dinner for six at El Gato Rojo in Breckenridge."

"Lucky him. Even I've heard of that restaurant."

"Lucky you too. Monday's my birthday, and Ryan said we should use the certificate for that."

Ashley smiled. "And you're asking me and Cole?"

"And Ellen and Ben. The Happy Tails Puppy Brigade plus Ryan. I checked with Cole first because his work schedule changes sometimes. I'll call Ellen and Ben next."

"El Gato Rojo means The Red Cat, right? I heard that was the chef's nickname in culinary school because he kept sneaking red chilis into everything."

Holly laughed. "I'm going to check out their menu later so I know what to order."

"I'll do that too," Ashley said, thinking she should also go back to Eagle's Nest Gifts to buy another little Navajo pottery piece as a birthday gift for Holly.

Holly suddenly sounded solemn. "You know, Ashley, I keep thinking about Ed Warner's last words."

El Gato Rojo was forgotten as "Danesle see skits" and a dying man filled Ashley's mind.

"I heard it a bit differently than you." Holly cleared her throat. "I heard Dane slesee skits. Or I thought I did."

Ashley leaned back into the couch cushions. "I keep going over those words too, trying to find sense in them."

"We both heard 'Dane' as the first syllable, right?"

"Which is one of the things that makes no sense. Where's there a Danish person in all this?"

"His boss isn't Danish, is he?"

Ashley pictured Oliver Ridley. "He's big and very dark. He didn't strike me as Scandinavian at all."

"I know I work too much with dogs, but I keep thinking Great Dane."

Ashley grinned. "Me too, but if we think of the Holmes household, there's a King Charles spaniel, a boxer, and a retriever. No Great Danes."

"Boxers are sort of like little Great Danes."

Ashley laughed out loud, making the sleeping Max twitch. "I think that's a bit of a stretch."

"Got a better idea?"

"No," Ashley admitted. "So you heard 'Dane slesee skits,' like 'Dane' was a stand-alone word. Then 'slesee.'"

"Whatever that means. I keep repeating it in my mind, expecting something to come clear."

"Nothing?"

Holly sighed. "Nothing. And you heard 'Danesle see skits' with 'see' as a stand-alone word. If that's what he said, did he mean 'see' as in using your eyes? Or did he see something?"

"At least we both heard 'skits.'"

"Or did we?" Holly asked. "What if he said 'sees kits' or 'slesees kits'? Does MarleyHolmes make kits of some kind?"

"They design software for farms and ranches. These days it's probably downloaded electronically, no kits required."

"Oh!" Holly's voice was full of excitement. "What if it wasn't 'sees' as in using your eyes, but 'seize' as in grabbing something from someone?"

"Holly, that's brilliant."

Holly deflated. "But 'seizing kits' still doesn't make sense."

Ashley had to agree. "The poor man was very ill, dying, and articulation wasn't his priority."

"I hope the police are doing better at this puzzle solving than we are."

Hoping to brighten Holly's mood, Ashley decided to change the subject. "Guess what? Kristin took me to watch the kids film their shows today. Very impressive. You should have seen the Winston Churchill outfit on an English bulldog."

"Was it Archie?" Holly asked, perking up. "He's one of my favorite clients."

"Yep. And there was a ski outfit for a Newfoundland. I bet Zeus would look great in it."

Holly chuckled. "When Zeus learns to ski, I'll consider it. You know, I heard some interesting stuff about the Andersen kids the other day at work. I was finishing a standard poodle for one customer when the next client arrived with her Lhasa apso. Both dog owners brought along their teens, local high school students who know Garrett and Rani. The poodle's owner was one of those sharp-tongued girls, critical and jealous. The other was a nice girl who clearly didn't want any part of the conversation but didn't know how to get out of it."

"Some things never change," Ashley mused. "Like types of teenagers."

"No kidding," Holly agreed. "So the mean girl says, 'Don't you love it that Garrett's become such a loser?' The nice girl said, 'I always liked Garrett. He's so cute.' A little apologetic, but she stood up for him. And the other girl said, 'Yeah, but cute can't save him now.'"

"How awful."

"Agreed. And she goes on, 'And that Rani. Who does she think she is, strutting around like some celebrity?' The nice girl cleared her throat. 'I think she is a celebrity.' The mean girl snorted. 'At least she's not a loser.'"

For perhaps the first time Ashley felt a twinge of sympathy for Garrett. "I get the impression that Garrett thinks of himself as a loser too. He tried really hard with his program today, but there was no zip, no zing. And he's smart enough to know it."

"Poor Kristin."

"He thinks Mark married her for her money." Ashley had never spoken to anyone about what she had overheard, but it wasn't as if Garrett had made any secret of his feelings.

"I haven't seen them together much, but I've never gotten that impression. They genuinely love each other," Holly said. "I bet Garrett saw himself as the man of the house after his dad died. Now he sees Mark as an interloper trying to take his place."

"The tension in that house makes me sad for all of them, especially Kristin and Mark."

"They're ready, honey," Ryan said in the background on Holly's end of the line.

"Coming," Holly called. "I've got to go, Ashley. Ryan brought in the burgers he was grilling. Think about El Gato Rojo instead of the

Ed Warner puzzle or the Marley Meadows household. You'll have an easier time falling asleep tonight."

After she hung up, Ashley took Holly's advice. She grabbed her laptop and went to the El Gato Rojo website. Based on the enticing food photos on the landing page alone, she knew she'd be skipping lunch Monday so she'd be super hungry for dinner.

After she had narrowed down her menu selections to a top five, she clicked over to Baldini Technologies's website. What she read drained some of her excitement about Monday. If she understood correctly, Baldini dealt in software designed to help ranchers manage their land and herds, just like MarleyHolmes.

She thought of all those pages of code. What if they contained proprietary information that belonged to Mark's company, had been stolen, and were being sent to the competition? What if somehow she had inadvertently gotten involved in industrial espionage? A shiver passed through her.

She picked up her little clay turtle and ran her finger over its exaggerated shell. The whimsy of it calmed her. Tomorrow, she'd talk to Bette and see what she thought about the code and the address. Her mind settled, she managed to relax for the rest of the evening.

But a phone call at five o'clock Sunday morning disrupted her plan.

15

"**D**r. Hart, it's Lowell Andersen." The man's usually calm voice was tight with concern.

Ashley sat up and shoved her hair out of her eyes. "What's wrong?"

"Remember Skye, that mare I told you about yesterday? Well, she's here."

In the background, Ashley could hear a distressed horse crying out. "I'll be right there."

She threw on some clothes, took a few minutes to feed Max and let him out, then hurried out the door, leaving the Dalmatian inside since a frightened horse could pose a danger to him.

Day hadn't yet broken as she sped up the drive to Marley Meadows, and lights were on in the barn and yard. Three people were gathered outside the paddock while a horse galloped around the inside perimeter, her breath steaming in the cold morning air.

Ashley recognized Lowell as one of the onlookers, so she joined him by the paddock. Skye was a beauty, all black except for a white blaze and white socks on her front legs. Her mane and tail blew out behind her as she ran.

Lowell watched the mare with worried eyes. "She showed up earlier than we expected, around ten last night, doped to the gills for travel. I'd gone home, as had the rest of the staff. Only Henry was here." He indicated the person next to him, the gangly boy Ashley had seen filling in dirt holes yesterday.

"He seemed like a sleepy old thing." Henry spread his hands.

"They led him—"

"Her," Lowell interrupted. "She's a mare. A she, not a he."

Henry cleared his throat and tried again. "They led her out of the trailer, helped me get her in her stall, and left. She was so lethargic we practically had to push her."

The horse thundered by in another of her countless circles. Steam poured from her nostrils and her body. She ran the paddock once more, then stopped, staring out over the predawn darkness. She called, then listened, ears pricked.

A couple of horses answered from the barn, but she paid no attention to them. They were not the voices she wanted to hear. She began running the fence again.

Henry frowned as he watched her. "I went to bed around eleven, and all was quiet." He pointed up at the barn. "I have a little apartment up there. At about three, I woke up hearing frantic whinnying and bumping and all kinds of noise. I came down to find her going nuts, throwing herself around the stall, trying to break free."

"He didn't know what to do, so he called me." Garrett leaned around Henry to continue the story. He must have seen Ashley's surprise and misinterpreted the cause. He gave Henry a hearty thwack on the back. "Henry and I are longtime buds."

Her surprise was that Garrett had pulled himself out of bed on a cold night for a distressed horse. It didn't fit the picture she had of him.

"Garrett came to the barn right away," Henry said. "In the meantime, all her noise and agitation were stirring up the other horses. I could hear them moving around."

Garrett nodded. "I decided we had to get her out of her stall before she hurt herself. The main thing that kept her from real injury was that Henry had left her clipped to the wall."

"I was supposed to have taken off her bridle and given her freedom in her stall." Henry shuddered. "But horses make me nervous, so I left her tied up."

Ashley frowned. This boy was working at a ranch?

Garrett gave his friend the side eye. "For once it's good you didn't do what you should have."

"Never thought I'd hear you say that," Henry muttered.

"Don't get used to it." Garrett climbed to sit on the paddock rail. "It allowed me to get near her and get a lead on her. We brought her out here and called Uncle Lowell."

"They told me she was difficult, and they were right," Lowell said. "We shouldn't have taken her, but would anyone listen to me?" He heaved a long-suffering sigh.

As she watched Skye, Ashley could detect nothing wrong with her gait or her general movement. She appeared to favor no body part as if in pain. She did seem disoriented and upset. That could be explained easily: The poor mare had woken up in a strange place with no notion of where she was or how she got there.

"What do you know about where she came from, Lowell?" she asked.

Lowell rested his arms on the top rail. "I know this is the third stable in six months. A ranch in the southern part of the state sold her to a woman who wanted to own a horse. She had a small barn built for Skye, moved her in, and then had very little time for her. When the lady did want to ride, Skye was contentious and uncooperative."

Ashley was getting the picture. "So she went from being part of a herd to being solitary to being here, where she knows no one and recognizes nothing. Poor baby."

Lowell raised an eyebrow. "You think this carrying on doesn't have physical roots but psychological ones?"

Garrett watched her. "Like a panic attack?"

Ashley nodded. "At a guess, I'd say we've got acute separation anxiety. I'll need to check her over when I can get near her for a long enough time, but I don't see any indication of physical difficulty from here. She moves with ease and grace. It's her emotional distress we need to alleviate as quickly as possible."

"You're thinking separation anxiety because of the running the fence? The calling? The stopping and listening?" Garrett slipped off the rail and into the paddock. "She's searching for her herd, her family."

Ashley glanced at him in surprise. He had read the symptoms accurately.

"I need to get near her." Ashley opened her medical bag to retrieve a tranquilizer.

Skye stopped again and stood listening. Ashley's heart contracted. Poor Skye. She'd lost everything and everyone she knew. Ashley had no idea whether she'd been part of a genuine herd that pastured together, had been companion to a single horse that she shared a barn with, or maybe even had a person who had been her security. But if her guess was correct, Skye had lost whatever security she had when she was put in that solitary barn like a prisoner. Horses were social animals and did much better with companions.

Garrett slowly moved closer to Skye, who watched him from the corner of her eye. He held out a hand with a horse treat. "Hey, sweet girl. Life's hard, isn't it?" he murmured. "I get it. I lost someone I loved too."

Skye watched Garrett approach. Her nostrils flared as she smelled the treat.

"What's going on here?" Kristin's voice cut the night as she strode to the paddock and stopped beside Ashley. She must have come straight from her bed. She wore Wellington boots with a nightgown, which fluttered under a puffy jacket. She hadn't taken time to brush her hair.

"Hey, Kris." Lowell gave her a nod of acknowledgment. "I didn't wake you and Mark because I figured Mark needs his rest."

Kristin raised an eyebrow. "But you woke Garrett?"

"Not me," Lowell said. "Henry did that."

"Hi, Mrs. Andersen." Henry waved.

"It's Mrs. Holmes, Henry," Kristin corrected gently, but most of her attention was on Garrett as he moved closer and closer to the twitchy horse. "Lowell?"

"I've got him covered. Come on, Henry." Lowell began moving along the outside of the rails, shadowing Garrett. Henry followed rather reluctantly.

Garrett continued to move closer and closer to Skye, who watched him as if trying to decide what she should do about this tall kid advancing on her. Was he friend or foe? Should she flee or fight?

"Kristin, I understand your late husband was a horse whisperer," Ashley said.

Her friend gave a little laugh. "I don't know about that, but he had a wonderful rapport with his animals."

"Do you think Garrett inherited his father's gift?" Ashley asked, but the answer to her question seemed obvious.

In the paddock, Skye took a few steps to meet Garrett, her sides still heaving, and buried her nose in his palm. As she gobbled the treat, he clipped the lead to her bridle, then ran a gentle hand down her neck. "That's a good girl," Garrett murmured.

"Awesome, Garrett," Henry called. "That was so cool."

Now it was Ashley's turn. She entered the paddock, careful to keep an eye on hooves and teeth. Just because the mare wasn't fighting Garrett didn't mean she'd accept anyone else.

"Keep talking to her, Garrett," Ashley said. "She's still wired."

He did so, and Ashley slipped the shot into the horse's flank. Skye's skin rippled as if she'd been bitten by a fly, but she continued to listen to Garrett, apparently mesmerized by his soothing tone.

"Take her in the barn, Garrett." Ashley pointed. "Slowly walk her through, letting her see the others stabled there. Show her that she has a new herd, at least for the time being. Slow and easy. We need to blanket her too, or she'll get a chill. When the tranquilizer takes effect, I'll check her out."

"Come on, Skye, pretty girl." Garrett ran a hand down her neck several times in that soothing motion the mare seemed to love. "Let's go meet your new friends."

As the young man and the calming horse disappeared into the barn, Ashley smiled. "He's going to have to spend lots of time with her over the next days, maybe weeks, to get her comfortable here," she said when she'd rejoined the others near the fence. "The sad thing is that if she gets comfortable here with the other horses and with Garrett, the separation anxiety will return when her owner takes her home to be solitary again."

"Garrett will fix her," Henry said confidently. "I've seen him do marvelous things with horses."

"Really?" Kristin seemed floored.

"Sure," Henry said. "They love him, and he loves them."

So why, Ashley wondered, was he fixing his future on dogs?

"Come inside for a cup of coffee, Ashley." Kristin gestured toward the house. "No sense staying out here in the cold while you wait for the tranquilizer to take effect."

"Thanks, I'd like that," Ashley said.

Lowell jerked a thumb toward the barn. "Since you're awake, Henry, you can start mucking out the stalls. And no cutting corners. I want everything neat and tidy. Lots of clients will be visiting today. Make it look good. Fresh water, fresh food, fresh straw."

"Yes, sir." If Henry's shoulders drooped any further, they'd be dragging on the ground.

Minutes later, Ashley was sitting with Kristin and Mark at the kitchen table sipping very good coffee and nibbling on toasted bagels.

"How are you feeling about surgery tomorrow, Mark?" Ashley asked.

"I'm not too worried about the surgery," he answered. "It's being stuck in the hospital overnight and the possibility they'll stick me in a wheelchair for my recovery. I hope for my wife's sake that I get a boot. The last thing she'll want is to push me around in a wheelchair."

She wagged a finger at him. "You know I wouldn't mind."

Rani ran into the room. "Mom, I need your advice."

"You're up early for a Sunday morning." Kristin rose and got a plate. "Bagel?"

"Maybe later." She held up a piece of blue material. "What do you think of this fabric? It's for Ava."

"Ava's the papillon," Kristin told Ashley.

Rani continued, "I really wanted to make something for Ma Belle—"

"She's a springer spaniel," Kristin explained.

"—but I need more fabric and I can't find the other piece of the material." Rani reached the table and tossed the scrap down in frustration.

Ashley blinked in disbelief as she examined the blue-and-gold brocade. "I have it."

Rani, Kristin, and Mark stared at her.

"How could you have it?" Rani asked. "It was in my sewing room."

"The kittens I've been trying to place arrived on my front porch in a basket lined with that material," Ashley answered.

Kristin and Mark exchanged glances, and Mark shook his head. "One step forward and three steps back," he said.

"He did well with the horse situation," Kristin said.

"What horse?" Rani asked.

"A new one that Dr. Hart thinks is suffering from separation anxiety," Kristin told her.

"Horses get anxiety?" Rani seemed fascinated.

Ashley nodded. "And they can suffer panic attacks. I think that was Skye's problem this morning. But about that material." She tapped the fabric. "Who put the kittens on my step?"

"Someone who didn't want to drive all the way to Fluffy Friends Adoption and Rescue and picked a nearby house instead." Kristin shook her head. "He's going to drive me crazy."

"I wanted to keep them all." Rani slathered cream cheese on a bagel. "I mean, really. Can a ranch have too many cats?"

"My friend Adrienne volunteers at Fluffy Friends, and she assured me they have a waiting list for kittens. They'll all go to good homes." Kristin gave a little snort. "Or they would have if we'd gotten them there."

"I told you the gap year thing was a bad idea." Rani got a glass from the cabinet and poured herself some orange juice. "That material would have been just right for Ma Belle. It'll be cute on Ava because everything is cute on her, but it would have been dynamite on Ma Belle." She grabbed the brocade and wandered off, juice, bagel, and material in hand, muttering under her breath about "that boy."

"You want the material back?" Ashley called after her.

"After five kittens have lived in it?" Rani's tone was pure disgust. "I think not."

There was a knock at the patio door. Kristin answered, and Ashley heard Henry's voice say, "Garrett said to tell Dr. Hart Skye's ready."

She followed Henry to the barn and spent considerable time evaluating Skye. As she'd expected, she found no physical issues. She gave Skye plenty of affection, which the mare seemed to appreciate. When Garrett walked into the stall, however, Skye melted—much, Ashley thought, like the female audience members who had once felt the same when they saw the young man on screen. He clearly had his father's gift with horses. Would he ever realize it—and capitalize on it?

Monday brought a busy morning at work, including a big black dog of indeterminate lineage who'd decided to defend his territory from a porcupine. As he slept off his surgery, an older lady came in and adopted the little gray kitten.

"Company I don't have to walk." The woman grinned at Ashley. "Win-win."

If her keen purring was any indication, the little gray, nestled in her new owner's arms, obviously agreed.

It was already one o'clock before Ashley had time to breathe. The waiting room was empty. "I've got to run a couple of errands, Ellen. I won't be long."

Ellen waved a hand. "Take your time. Unless there's a life in peril, I won't call you."

Ashley's first stop was Eagle's Nest Gifts. She went directly to the shelf of Navajo pottery and there sat another turtle, only this one featured the natural reddish tone often found in Navajo handiwork. She flipped it over, and sure enough, it was signed by Margaret White Bear.

"Isn't it the cutest?" The girl at the checkout counter wrapped the turtle carefully in tissue paper and nestled it inside a colorful shopping bag. "We sell tons of them."

Ashley took the bag with a smile, but she felt oddly disappointed to know that lots of people had her little turtle. It had been such a kick thinking she and Holly would own matching one-of-a-kind pottery. *Oh, well.*

"They're made by this enclave of Navajo artisans in northwest New Mexico," the clerk went on. "They raise money to fund youth enrichment activities through the sale of their pottery as well as corporate sponsors like MarleyHolmes Technologies."

"That's wonderful," Ashley said, feeling better about how special her turtle was. She also realized MarleyHolmes's connection to the organization explained how Bette knew Margaret White Bear. "I'll have to find out more about them."

Coincidentally, MarleyHolmes Technologies was Ashley's next stop. She stepped through the double glass doors of the large building into a lobby done in navy and gray with a massive granite desk at the rear. Artistic photos of the Rockies in minimalist frames hung on the walls.

"I'm here to see Bette DeVane," she told the burly man behind the desk.

He glowered at her. "Is she expecting you?"

Ashley studied his stern face. If it wasn't for the MarleyHolmes blazer he wore over his black jeans and T-shirt, she might have mistaken him for a celebrity bodyguard. His broad shoulders and gruff attitude indicated he knew exactly how to protect himself and anyone else he was responsible for.

Thank goodness she'd called ahead. "Yes, she's expecting me. Ashley Hart."

The man's formidable expression melted into a sweet smile that somehow made him appear even more intimidating. He gestured to a cluster of sleek leather-and-chrome chairs. "Have a seat, please. I'll let her know you're here."

Ashley took a chair and waited, the folder of mystery pages from her printer resting in her lap.

"She's on her way," the muscle-bound receptionist called. "May I get you some water while you wait?"

"Thanks, but no." To Ashley's surprise, she felt nervous. Was she being foolish bothering Bette? Probably. But, she reminded herself, it was better to be cautious than risk something nefarious happening. If she could make a difference or stop a tragedy and didn't say anything . . .

A door at the rear of the lobby opened, and a young woman wearing slacks and a royal blue MarleyHolmes sweater over a white collared shirt walked through. "Hey, Bubba." She gave him a little wave.

"Eloise, my favorite genius." He grinned, then nodded toward Ashley.

Eloise crossed the lobby to Ashley, who stood. "Dr. Hart? I'm Eloise Goff, one of the many geeks who work here."

"Pleasure to meet you." Ashley decided she liked Eloise. Self-identifying geeks were some of her favorite people.

"Ms. DeVane asked me to bring you to her office. Follow me, please."

They walked to the door Eloise had come through, where she swiped a security card and entered a six-digit code in a keypad. The door unlocked with a soft buzz.

"The code changes daily." Eloise shrugged, pushing through the door. "We're a bit security conscious. Makes visitors think important stuff happens here."

"Doesn't it?" Ashley asked.

Eloise merely grinned. She led Ashley down a long hall that ended with two offices opposite each other. The door on the right was closed, its nameplate reading *Mark Holmes, CEO*. Eloise turned to the left, marked *Bette DeVane, VP Operations*. Eloise knocked on the partially open door. "Dr. Hart's here, Ms. DeVane."

"Come on in, Ashley." Bette came to the door, a smile on her face. She was elegant as always in black slacks, a white silk shirt, and a cropped black-and-white checked jacket. No company sweater for her.

Ashley suddenly felt self-conscious about every wrinkle and dog hair to be found on the navy scrubs she wore under her winter coat. "Hi, Bette."

"Thank you, Eloise." Bette gave a dismissive wave.

The young woman shot Ashley a farewell smile, then disappeared down the hall.

The farther Eloise had led Ashley from the impressive lobby, the more utilitarian the building's decor had become—until she entered Bette's office, where the woman's personal elegance was reflected in her surroundings.

Done in gray-blues and white, the office had a beautiful wooden desk arranged so that every time Bette glanced up, she looked out a window onto a grassy lawn that backed up to a swathe of forest. Currently, three elk grazed on the grass while the evergreens behind them swayed in the breeze. Scenic watercolors hung on the walls, and groupings of plants added warmth to the room. Professional but inviting. Very vice presidential. Very Bette.

"Have a seat." Bette indicated a grouping of two chairs and a sofa. Ashley sank into a very comfortable chair upholstered in a blue tweed that matched the wall.

"Can I get you some coffee or tea?"

Ashley held up a hand. "No thanks. I won't take that much of your time. I'm sure you're busy, especially with Mark out, and I have to get back to the clinic for office hours."

Bette nodded and sat on the white leather couch. "Never too busy for a friend."

Ashley smiled and held out the folder. "My printer spit this out without my say-so the other night."

Bette leafed through the papers. When she came to the last sheet, the Baldini label, her brows rose. "Baldini? Really?"

"The name means something to you?"

"I should think so. He's our chief competitor. Our archenemy. I worry that if Mark's not careful, we'll be the victims of an unfriendly takeover at their hands."

Ashley blinked. Another Mark jab? "Speaking of Mark, have you heard anything about his surgery?"

Bette gathered all the papers in a neat stack, placing the label on top. "Kris called about an hour ago. The procedure went well and he's in recovery."

"Great." Ashley pointed at the papers in Bette's lap. "So they're not evidence of industrial espionage? No important proprietary information being passed to the enemy?"

Bette was amused by the idea. "None at all. The coding is what created the label. Why the coding printed out rather than just the label I don't know, nor why it printed out on your printer. Very strange, but not anything to be worried about."

Ashley stood. "Thanks for explaining it to me."

Bette set the folder on the couch and stood too. "Let me walk you out."

Ashley held out her hand.

Bette shook it.

Ashley grinned. "I was reaching for the folder."

Bette chuckled. "Of course you were." She picked it up and passed it over.

They walked to the door. As they opened it, Bette's phone rang. She frowned toward it.

"Go ahead and answer it," Ashley said. "I can walk myself out. It's only down the hall." She hesitated. "Unless I need you to swipe me out."

"You can get out very easily. It's getting in that we make hard."

The phone rang again.

"Go on," Ashley said. "I know this is a busy time for you, what with the new product about to release."

Bette nodded and moved toward her desk. "Thanks for understanding."

Ashley started down the hall. A door on her left opened, and Chaz Romaine, the VP of IT, stepped into the hall, brow furrowed as usual. Ashley tried for a quick sidestep, but he still barreled into her. She staggered and her folder went flying, scattering papers everywhere.

"I'm so sorry!" A startled Chaz grabbed Ashley's arm to steady her. "Are you all right?"

"I'm fine," Ashley said.

Chaz studied her in surprise. "You're the vet for Mark's dog, right?" He was obviously wondering what she was doing in the depths of the MarleyHolmes building.

"I am. I had a meeting with Bette."

"Ah." He bent and began gathering her papers. He glanced at them without much interest—until he picked up the Baldini label. He waved it at her, his frown even deeper than usual. "What's this?"

"I have no idea. My printer printed it without my input." She indicated all the papers. "I had no idea whether they were important, so I came to see Bette to ask her what she thought."

He continued to eye her suspiciously.

"I know she's something of a computer geek. Or at least she was before going into management." Ashley felt foolish explaining herself, but she understood his distrust, his uncertainty. A lot was at stake for MarleyHolmes.

"You're not in touch with Baldini, are you? Maybe Dominic himself or someone who works there?"

"Not at all, believe me. I don't know a Dominic. I'm a veterinarian. I don't even know what you do here except in the broadest terms."

"Can I keep these?" Chaz indicated the papers. "I'd like to try to trace them."

Ashley's brows rose. "You can find where they came from?"

Chaz shrugged. "I can try. Depends how much encryption I run into."

"But you think it could be important."

Chaz shook his head like a fighter who'd had one too many blows. "Maybe. Maybe not. But Mark hired Ed Warner for some reason, and he's dead. What if somebody else is next?"

16

Ashley sat in her office trying to read a technical journal with Patch to keep her company. The little rascal was adjusting to his newly solitary existence well, romping around the clinic as if he owned the place. Unlike poor Skye, Patch wasn't distressed by the separation from his companions. While cats liked each other and could be sociable, most were also happy to be alone . . . although today Patch seemed eager for attention from Ashley.

He leaped into her lap and sat on her journal. She scratched him behind the ears, and he leaned into her hand. "We need to find you a forever family, little one. You like people."

He answered by jumping to her desk and scattering the pile of papers Ellen had carefully left for her. He signaled his pleasure at the chaos he'd created by grooming his back leg in the middle of the mess. Ashley grabbed him around the middle and set him on the floor. "Be good or you'll go back in your crate."

He sniffed and chased an imaginary mouse under the desk.

Ellen knocked on her door and stuck her head in. "Dr. Hart, you have a visitor."

Dr. Hart? How unusually formal. When Ellen waggled her brows, Ashley knew something was up.

A man walked in, and Ashley recognized the deep-set eyes and heavy brows immediately. He wasn't frowning as he'd been the last time she saw him but rather smiling and radiating charm.

"Thank you, Ellen." As Ellen excused herself, closing the door behind her, Ashley stood and offered her visitor the chair on the opposite side of her desk. "Mr. Ridley."

Oliver seemed surprised. "You know me?"

"I was at Mark's house when you came on Saturday," Ashley explained.

He sank into the chair. "I'm sorry. I don't remember meeting you there."

"No reason you should. I'm not part of MarleyHolmes. I was there to tend to their dogs."

"That's right. Mrs. Holmes raises show dogs."

"She does." Ashley returned to her own seat. "What can I do for you, Mr. Ridley?"

He startled and peeked under the desk. "There's a cat chasing my shoelaces."

"He's waiting for adoption. I've been calling him Patch."

Patch must have decided he liked Oliver Ridley because he was suddenly in the man's lap. Ashley rose to take the kitten and return him to his crate, but Oliver raised his hand.

"He's fine." He ran a hand down the cat's back. "And aren't you a handsome boy?"

Ashley felt a surge of hope. "You wouldn't want—"

Oliver shook his head. "Sorry. All full up on pets. I already have a dog and two cats. The cats are siblings, and they'd go nuts if I tried to bring in an interloper."

Poor Patch. At least he didn't know he'd been rejected.

Oliver crossed his legs, absently petting Patch. He eyed Ashley. "You found him."

She took a deep breath. As soon as she'd seen Oliver come through the door, she'd known why he was here. Still, it was a difficult memory to revisit. "I did."

"Tell me."

As she recounted the story, Oliver listened carefully, as if he were memorizing her words.

"Didn't the police tell you all this?" she asked when she was about halfway through.

"Firsthand is always better than secondhand," he said. "Often pieces of information emerge that the middleman didn't catch or didn't realize were important."

Ashley admitted that truth and told her tale all the way to the end. When she finished, Oliver sat forward. "He said what?"

Ashley spread her hands. "I know. It makes no sense. 'Danesle see skits.' Or as my friend who was with me heard it, 'Dane slesee skits.' Or maybe it was 'Dane slesees kits.' Or 'seize' instead of 'sees.'"

Oliver's brow furrowed again, but not in anger as it had on Saturday. He was contemplating the many permutations of Ed Warner's last words. At one point he shook his head as if he was as unable to solve the puzzle as she.

After some time, Oliver seemed to give up. Ashley thought he might be ready to leave, but instead, he sat back in his chair, continuing to pet a now-sleepy Patch. "I run an investigation business with my partner, Bob Baker," Oliver said. "Most of our work is not dangerous. It's things like following wayward spouses, tracing bail skippers, checking into suspect financials. The fastest-growing section of RBI is cybersecurity, which is a lot of tracing and gathering evidence against illegal hackers. We'll even break into theoretically secure servers to find the weak spots and then develop a plan to correct them if that's what a client wants."

Ashley nodded, having read about hackers and identity thieves.

Oliver continued. "Then there's industrial espionage, where one company tries to steal another's proprietary information and programs. That's what this case appears to be. Or at least what Mark Holmes thinks it is. MarleyHolmes information has become public without consent in the past. When Ed came here, the plan was to find the leak and tighten security so this doesn't happen with the super-secret program about to go to market."

"I know they're all stressed about the new product launch," Ashley said.

"Embezzlers and secret sellers usually aren't violent people. Ed should not have been in danger." Sorrow filled Oliver's face. "I sent him here, which makes me somewhat responsible."

Ashley's heart went out to him. "You couldn't have foreseen what happened, Mr. Ridley."

"Thank you." But he didn't appear convinced. He stood, still holding Patch, and began to pace the small office. "I went back to Denver on Saturday after talking to Mark Holmes, but I couldn't stay there. I had to come back. And I'm staying until I find out what happened."

"I'm sure the police are doing their best," Ashley said.

"Yes, but they didn't know Ed. They have no personal stake in this." He stopped and looked at Ashley. "At least they did one thing right by sending Ed to the big lab. They got the report back on the poison. It's tetrodotoxin, which is easy to get if you have the right connections."

Ashley couldn't help but grimace. Tetrodotoxin, found in puffer fish, was highly lethal. Oliver was right—it was fortunate that Ed Warner had been sent to the toxicologists at El Paso County Coroner's Office in Colorado Springs. They'd done the right tests and found their evidence. There was now confirmation of what everyone suspected.

Murder.

Patch squirmed a bit in Oliver's arms and jumped to the ground, where he attacked one of Oliver's shoelaces again. The investigator watched the kitten with a small smile.

"You sure you don't want Patch?" Ashley asked.

"Wish I could, but I can't. He is a great fella, though."

"You know an RBI thumb drive arrived on my doorstep with Patch and his littermates, right?"

"So Chief Maloney told me. And I confirmed that it belonged to Ed. We've been working on breaking the encryption, as have the police."

"No luck yet, I assume?"

"Not yet. Ed had his own methods. For the encryption to be so deep, he must have found incriminating evidence he thought very substantial but wasn't yet ready to hand over to the authorities."

"I wonder what," Ashley said.

"Me too," Oliver walked to the door but paused with his hand on the knob. "There's got to be something we're missing. We just haven't thought of the right question to ask or the right place to search. But something happened between brunch at the Holmes house and Ed dying along the roadside several hours later."

"He had brunch with Mark and Kristin?" Ashley hadn't realized that.

Oliver nodded. "Then Ed and Mark had a meeting that was spent walking around outside so no one could overhear them. Ed called and told me all about it—the meeting, not the evidence. He was too excited about the opportunity to inspect the horses. He used to compete in Western dressage when he was young. He sent a text right before he left the ranch saying how fabulous the horses were. When he got his bonus for finding the culprit, he intended to buy one and board it at Marley Meadows. He said it was time to get back in the saddle."

There was a moment of silence while they both contemplated the sad fact that Ed had never made it back in the saddle. Then Oliver squared his shoulders and opened the door.

Ashley moved quickly to scoop up Patch before he could escape. "If I can help in any way, Mr. Ridley, let me know. I'm not sure what I can do, but I'm here."

The investigator glanced back at her. "You found the thumb drive, which may lead us to something. You tried to save Ed. You've been an enormous help already."

Ashley thought of one more thing that might be a lead for Oliver to follow. "That litter of kittens with the thumb drive in their basket came from Marley Meadows."

Oliver's gaze sharpened. "What? You're sure?"

"The fabric the little guys were wrapped in belonged to Rani Andersen."

"Thank you," Oliver said curtly, then stalked away as if he had a renewed mission.

With the mention of Marley Meadows, Ashley's thoughts turned to Sweetie—and her illness the previous week. Had the spaniel somehow come in contact with tetrodotoxin? Out of an abundance of concern, Ashley had sent a blood sample to the lab—now she had something specific to request they test for.

Sure, something completely different might have made Sweetie sick, but Ed Warner had visited Marley Meadows and died of tetrodotoxin poisoning mere days before Sweetie had taken ill at the same location—a coincidence with deadly implications.

17

Dinner at El Gato Rojo was all Ashley had hoped and more, starting as soon as she and her friends walked in. Realizing that little red cat stickers were hidden on menus, pictures, decorative tiles, floral arrangements, even the tissue holders in the ladies' room, they made a game of finding as many as they could. The restaurant claimed they had hidden thirty-five cats—changed weekly to discourage cheating—and if a diner found all of them, they received a free drink on their next visit. The trick was to find all of them without disturbing any of the other diners.

The best part of the evening was watching Holly enjoy the outing, from appreciating the warm, hacienda-style decor to selecting decadent appetizers and entrees, to beaming with joy when the waitstaff gathered around their table and sang "Happy Birthday" to her over an individual tres leches cake shaped like a cat.

"Can I count him?" Holly asked the server when the singing was done.

"I would," the woman answered.

And Holly loved the Navajo turtle. "I'll treasure it always," she told Ashley as she hugged it to her chest.

Ashley laughed. "You don't have to make a lifelong commitment to it. I'm happy you like it."

Over dessert, conversation veered to Ed Warner's murder, with Ashley sharing what she'd learned about Ed, MarleyHolmes, and Oliver Ridley.

"What do you think, Holly?" Ellen asked Holly. "I've heard all of Ashley's theories. What are yours?"

Holly paused with a bite of cake halfway to her mouth. "I do have a thought. We're assuming that poor man was killed because of something here in Aspen Falls or at MarleyHolmes. What if someone from Denver decided to misdirect everyone by committing the crime in our town?"

Ryan beamed at her. "I never thought of that, birthday girl. Good for you."

Holly flushed with pleasure at the praise. "Thanks, sweetie."

Ryan held up an index finger. "I have a theory too. What if he wasn't the real target?"

"What do you mean?" Ben asked as he sliced into his cinnamon-sugar churros.

"Let's assume it's a local crime," Ryan went on. "Who's the local who's raised the most contentious feelings?"

Ashley knew the answer, but she didn't want to voice it.

"Mark's unpopular at home." Cole added more cream to his coffee.

"Only with some." Ashley felt she had to say that for Kristin's sake.

"What about at work?" Ben asked.

"His decision to employ Ed Warner behind everyone's back certainly sounded unpopular," Holly said.

"I don't remember hearing anything bad about him before." Ellen stirred her coffee.

"The Marleys were and are important locally. The ranch and kennel, to say nothing of MarleyHolmes Tech, provide a lot of jobs. On top of that, Helen and Clint were my good friends, and I've known Kristin since she was a baby. I hear all the gossip about them."

"So Mark's the interloper." Ryan became thoughtful. "Where did he come from?"

Ellen gazed at the ceiling as she tried to remember. "I think Clint Marley found him in California, somewhere in Silicon Valley. I don't remember the company since its name meant nothing to me." She drew in a breath. "Well, what do you know?"

"What?" Holly asked as they all looked up.

"There's a red cat on the ceiling fan."

Ashley found it sitting on the corner of the blade. "That must be one of the cats that moves around. You wouldn't be able to see it in the summer when the fan is going."

"Good point," Cole agreed, then returned to the less fanciful topic of murder. "So Ryan, you think since Mark's the outsider, he was the target, and somehow Ed Warner was a mistake?"

"Maybe he ate or drank the wrong thing," Ben said.

"So we need to find out where he ate and drank Sunday." Holly set her fork down on her empty cake plate.

"Mr. Ridley told me this afternoon that Ed had brunch with Mark and Kristin on Sunday," Ashley said, realizing she'd forgotten that detail earlier.

"Just the three of them?" Ellen shook her head. "No murderer there."

"Why not?" Ryan asked.

"Well, Ed Warner's dead," she said. "If he was the murderer, he'd be the one alive."

"Irrefutable logic," Ben said with a smile.

Ellen made a face at him. "And neither Kristin nor Mark is a murderer. Kristin doesn't have a violent bone in her body. And why would Mark hire Warner and then kill him? It wasn't as if he found information against Mark."

"How do you know?" Ben leaned in, his dark eyes alight with excitement. "What if Warner discovered Mark was cooking the books? Or that Kristin was, and Mark killed Warner to protect Kristin? True love and all that." He grinned.

Ellen pointed her index finger at him. "Says the guy who doesn't have a girlfriend."

"By choice," Ben said. "And not for lack of you trying to set me up. But I have school to focus on, you know."

"It wasn't just Ed, Mark, and Kristin at that brunch, was it?" Cole asked. "The kids would have been there, if not at the table, at least in the house."

Ryan's eyes glittered. He was having a good time playing sleuth. "And we know Garrett doesn't like Mark. Right, Ashley?"

Ashley's loyalty to Kristin and her desire to solve this murder warred inside her brain. "I overheard Mark yelling at Garrett for speeding," she admitted. "And I've heard him and Kristin despairing of getting Garrett to do his chores."

Ben raised his eyebrows. "The rich kid has to do chores?"

"'The rich kid' is one frustrated young man," Ashley said. "Career tanking, evil stepdad, uncertain future."

"But you've got to admit," Ben said, "it's a big step from disliking your new stepfather to killing him."

"Which he didn't do," Ellen was quick to say.

"Don't worry, Ellen." Cole smiled at her. "We have no evidence. And where would he get the poison?"

"Where would anyone?" Holly shook her head. "I certainly wouldn't know how to get something like that, and I bet none of the rest of you would either." She glanced around the circle until she came to Ashley, then she adopted an impish expression. "Except for Ashley. Doctors can get anything. Everyone knows that."

"Hilarious." Ashley held out her palm. "I'll take the turtle back, please."

Holly clamped her hand over it protectively.

"There's someone we keep writing off as innocent." Ryan shifted uncomfortably. "What about Kristin? What if she killed Ed Warner to protect Mark?"

"We're back to the logic thing," Cole said. "Mark started the ball rolling by hiring Warner. If he needed protecting, he'd never have hired him."

Holly frowned. "Assuming the highly unlikely scenario that Kristin killed Warner to protect Mark, how would she know Mark needed protection? She doesn't work at MarleyHolmes. She doesn't know the company secrets."

"At least, not as far as we know." Cole toyed with the paper wrapper that had encircled his silverware. "What if she knows a lot more than we think? What if she has an inside source? It doesn't even have to be Mark."

"Bette, maybe?" Ashley said. "They're extremely close."

"But Bette's a company woman," Ellen said. "She's worked there her whole professional life and done very well for herself. Would she tell company business to anyone, even her best friend? Wouldn't that jeopardize her own future? If MarleyHolmes goes down or goes broke, so does Bette."

"There's another person we haven't talked about," Ryan put in. "Isn't there a daughter who's got a temper?"

"Rani." Ashley thought about the budding online celebrity. "She might have it in for her brother. She held him responsible for Sweetie's illness. If she was going to bump off anyone, I'd think it would be him."

A dark-haired man in a sharp suit approached their table. "Good evening. I'm Gabriel Vargas. I want to thank you for coming to dine with us tonight. Please come again and tell your friends what a wonderful time you had." He grinned at Holly. "And happy birthday to you."

"This has been such a fun night," she said. "Reminds me of my grandmother's cooking, but—aha!" She pointed at the little red cat that sat halfway down his tie. "I claim that cat. That's twenty-five."

"Wonderful," Gabriel said smoothly. "Good luck finding ten more." He gave a head bob and walked off.

Holly grinned as she put a hand on Ryan's arm. "I'd be happy to come back here again and actually pay for dinner, wouldn't you?"

Amusement twinkled in Ryan's eyes. "If you're paying, I'd love to tag along."

"Here's an idea we haven't discussed yet." Cole paused until he had everyone's attention. "Wouldn't the head of security at MarleyHolmes feel stabbed in the back by Mark hiring Warner? It makes it look as though Mark didn't trust the guy."

Ashley nodded. "That's Whit Carlson. He is unhappy."

"And how does the head of IT feel about Warner?" Ryan asked.

"Chaz Romaine is also upset, but he seems like a grumpy old bear of a man in general," Ashley said, though she reminded herself that he'd taken the coding papers to try and solve their mystery. "I met them both when I took Sweetie home. They were having a meeting with Mark."

"MarleyHolmes is a major software company about to release a new program," Ryan said. "Doesn't bringing in a cybersecurity specialist mean you don't trust your lead information technology person or security chief?"

Cole nodded agreement. "Maybe Warner found something on one of them that caused whoever it was to kill rather than risk exposure."

Holly held up her hand. "Enough murder discussion. It's my birthday, after all."

"Quite right." Ellen gestured to the turtle Ashley had gotten Holly. "Ashley, tell us more about this wonderful pottery."

Ashley did, and the conversation grew animated as everyone recounted their favorite souvenirs.

Half an hour later, Ellen sighed as she checked her watch. "It's getting late and we all have work tomorrow. I say we all search for more cats on our way out and give Holly any that we find."

"That's so sweet, Ellen. Thank you." Holly's bright smile brought everyone to their feet.

Searching carefully for cats hidden in murals and chandeliers, they made their way to the cloak room to reclaim their coats. Ashley carefully studied the counter, the doorframe, even the coat check tip basket, eyes peeled for another red cat. She started to hand her ticket to the attendant, then pulled it back.

"Aha!" On one side was the number assigned to her coat, but on the other was a colorful Mexican flower with a little red cat sitting in its center. She showed the attendant the ticket number, then handed it to Holly. "Happy birthday."

Sliding her arms into her coat, Ashley glanced around the room, wondering where the remaining cats were hiding. Her gaze caught on a handsome couple waiting to be seated. He was tall with prematurely silver hair and a black mustache. She was striking with a white streak slashing through her dark hair. He had his hand on the small of her back as he whispered something into her ear. She sent him an incandescent smile and playfully swatted his shoulder. He laughed.

Ashley nudged Ellen. "It's Bette."

"They make an attractive couple." Ellen studied him. "Handsome fellow."

"You don't know him?"

"Believe it or not, there are people in central Colorado I haven't met." Ellen studied Bette and her escort. "Somehow I don't think they'll be searching for red cats. Too preoccupied with each other."

"How nice for her that she's got a romantic interest. I feel like I should say hi to her, but I don't want to interrupt."

"Good call." Ellen tilted her head in their direction even as she turned away from them. "Check out the hand resting on her waist."

"Very familiar."

"Which hand is it?"

Ashley checked. "Left hand."

Ellen raised an eyebrow. "And what's on the third finger of that left hand?"

Ashley cringed. Why was Bette out to dinner—and acting so flirtatious—with a married man?

18

Ashley had just stepped from the shower Tuesday morning when her phone rang. She wrapped an oversize towel around herself to fend off goose bumps in the chill morning air and answered the call.

"Ashley? It's Bette."

The very person Ashley had been thinking about much of the night after seeing her at El Gato Rojo. "Good morning, Bette. What's up?"

"Do you still have kittens you're hoping to find homes for?"

Bette was interested in one of her kittens at six thirty in the morning? "I have one we're calling Patch because he's a tricolor of orange, gray, and white. He's really quite pretty, and he's a sweetheart. A little rambunctious."

"Sounds adorable," Bette said. "I'd like to meet him with the possibility of adopting him."

"Wonderful," Ashley said, although concerns nagged at her. While she loved when homeless pets found their forever home, she wasn't so sure about this match. Was curious, adventurous Patch a good fit for organized, sophisticated Bette? She supposed it was worth letting them meet. Perhaps opposites would attract. "He's at the clinic. Hours begin at two today."

"Can you bring him to my house this morning for me to meet?" Bette asked, sounding as if she hadn't heard what Ashley had said. "I'm working from home until noon."

Ashley hesitated.

"I know that's asking a lot." Bette was apologetic but firm. "But you know what things are like at MarleyHolmes right now. I'm overwhelmed, but I don't want to miss this opportunity."

Ashley found herself feeling unexpectedly cynical. Bette had time to go over an hour to Breckenridge for dinner with someone else's husband, but not to drive a few minutes to the clinic?

But if Patch could have a good home . . .

Certainly Bette could afford him, and she'd see he got the best care.

"I've got coffee and homemade coffee cake," Bette sang out.

Coffee cake did sound better than the granola bar Ashley had planned for breakfast. "Sure," she agreed. "How about if I stop by before I make a ranch call?"

"How soon do you think you'll be here?"

"Is forty-five minutes okay?"

"Sounds good. I'll have coffee and cake waiting."

While Ashley had been on the phone. Max had wandered into the bathroom and stared at her expectantly. She knew what he wanted, but she was trepidatious enough taking a tiny kitten to Bette's home, let alone a full-grown Dalmatian. "I wish you could come, buddy, but not this trip." She knelt and hugged him.

He rested his chin on her shoulder for a moment, then walked to the bedroom, where he climbed on her bed and flopped down with his head on her pillow. She loved that he always seemed to know what she was telling him, although she sometimes had to roll her eyes at the ensuing drama.

A short while later, Ashley pulled into Bette's driveway and studied the gorgeous one-story house as she parked. The sleek, contemporary building was all wood and stone with fascinating roof angles and lots of windows. It was as elegant and charming as Bette.

Ashley hesitated before getting out. She'd spent the drive trying to decide how to act when she saw Bette. She told herself she didn't know the full story, but still, seeing Bette with a married man made her stomach sour on behalf of an unwitting wife. Then again, Bette was such a wonderful friend to Kristin and her kids, and Ellen had nothing but good things to say about her. Didn't she deserve the benefit of the doubt?

Ashley climbed from the car with Patch in a travel carrier. "If this works out, pal, you are landing in clover," she told him. "But you've got to be good. No running around like a maniac—at least not until she falls in love with you."

As Ashley approached the front door, Bette threw it open with a big smile.

"Good morning, Ashley." Bette peered through the carrier's door at Patch. "Aren't you a pretty boy?"

Patch recognized a compliment when he heard one. He purred loudly.

Attaboy, Ashley thought. *Sell yourself.*

Ashley stepped into an entry hall the size of her living room. A marble-topped desk sat against the wall with a mirror above it. A gorgeous arrangement of flowers sat on the desk, reflected in the mirror and making the area glow with color. She blinked away the image of Patch hopping up onto the desk and sending the bouquet flying.

Bette held out her hand for Ashley's coat. Ashley set Patch's carrier on the floor and shrugged out of it, sliding her scarf into the sleeve as she withdrew her arm. Bette hung it in a closet large enough to handle the coats for a dinner party of fifty.

"Come on back to the kitchen." Bette led the way.

Ashley picked up Patch and followed. She glanced into the living room as she passed. It was a symphony of cream and blues with pops of citron in cushions and throws. A piano painted Wedgwood blue sat against the far wall.

"I didn't know you played." Ashley nodded toward it. "You are a woman of many talents."

Bette made a face. "Don't be too impressed. When I bought it, I planned to take lessons. I always wanted to know how to play." She ran her fingers up and down an imaginary keyboard, then shrugged. "Somehow I never got around to the lessons. Too busy, you know? But I like how it fits in the room."

"It certainly makes a statement," Ashley said, though in her mind she was watching Patch trot across the keys, making his own kind of music.

The kitchen was sleek white with stainless steel appliances, the only color a bowl of green apples in the middle of the island. White cabinets, white marble countertops, white island with white stools. Everything was so ordered and clean, Ashley wondered if Bette ever cooked here.

Then her nose picked up the delicious smell of a cinnamon cake in the oven.

A large window filled the far wall, the landscape of leafless aspens stretching to the mountains in the distance.

"What a view, Bette," Ashley said. "It must be absolutely beautiful when the aspens change color."

"I enjoy it." Bette started a coffee maker, then patted the top of the island. "Let me meet this handsome boy. You can set him here."

Ashley set the carrier down and unzipped it. She put her hand up in an attempt to keep Patch from streaking out like a prisoner making a desperate bid for freedom. *Slow and easy, buddy. Slow and easy.*

Canny boy that he was, he emerged one step at a time, all the while gazing at Bette with his beautiful, pumpkin-colored eyes.

"Oh, he's wonderful," Bette cooed, already smitten.

As if to reinforce her reaction, Patch padded over to her outstretched hand and rubbed against her palm.

Ashley bit back a laugh. How she loved animals. They were so smart.

They could read a situation and make the most of it—if they felt like it. Dogs usually played nice. But with cats, you never knew.

Bette picked Patch up, and he leaned into her, purring.

Ashley relaxed and slid onto one of the stools. She didn't have to sell Patch. He was doing a fine job himself.

A few minutes later the oven timer dinged.

"Sorry, baby." Bette set Patch on the floor. "I've got to get the coffee cake out."

Patch sat like a little gentleman.

Bette grabbed a white oven mitt from a drawer, then opened the oven door. "Ashley, he's perfect." But as soon as the last word was out of her mouth, Patch took off back the way they'd come.

The real Patch had come out to play.

Bette laughed as she watched him go. "Don't worry. He can't hurt anything."

Ashley went cold as she pictured all the lovely—and likely expensive—objets d'art throughout Bette's home. Patch was a climber, a jumper. Catastrophe was inevitable.

"I'd better see what he's up to." Ashley started to follow.

"I'm really not worried about it," Bette insisted.

"I am."

Ashley made her way toward the front door, tracing the route Patch had taken. As she reached a divide in the hall, Patch streaked from the front of the house down one wing.

"Come here, you," she hissed. "You're going to kill your chances."

Patch, of course, ignored her and darted through a doorway. Ashley stopped at the threshold of what she recognized as a guest bedroom. Patch leaped onto a bed covered with a satin comforter, pushing his way through the pile of pillows leaning against the headboard. They went flying off the other side, as did he.

Ashley checked the satin for pulls from Patch's claws while she tried to arrange the pillows as they'd been. She knew she was failing, but at least there were no snags in the fabric. Patch returned to the doorway, where he sat watching, his tail flicking from side to side, and she got the sense he was laughing at her.

"You think this is funny?" She moved toward him and shooed him out. "Back to the kitchen with you."

He took off in the opposite direction, heading farther down the hall, and raced through the next open door he found. Ashley groaned at the sight of the beautiful master bedroom he'd invaded. It was as elegant as the rest of the house, done in soft grays and violets. She couldn't help but admire a gorgeous throw at the end of the bed, which appeared to be cashmere. She was reaching out to touch it when a crash echoed through the room.

Patch had jumped on the bureau, where he was nosing his way through a collection of perfume bottles that, until two seconds ago, had been artfully arranged there. What his head didn't knock over, his tail pushed aside.

"Patch!" Ashley lunged for him. He gave his tail one last flick, which sent a pretty pink perfume bottle to the floor, where it bounced onto the rug without its stopper falling out, thank goodness.

He jumped to the floor. Before she'd even changed directions, he'd pulled the beautiful throw to the floor and burrowed under it. She grabbed the throw only to have him squirm out the other side. He made for the door. She picked up the throw and tossed it back on the bed, intending to come back and straighten it later.

She hurried to the hall and caught a glimpse of a white-tipped tail disappearing into a room with its door barely cracked open. He must have butted against it and loosened a not-quite-caught latch.

"Patch!" she hissed. "Get out of there."

The answer was soft thuds. He was climbing something.

Ashley glanced down the hall, but Bette was still busy in the kitchen. Feeling she was invading Bette's privacy—doors were usually closed for a reason—she pushed the door open far enough to peer in.

Tan corrugated boxes were piled all around the room. Some stacks nearly reached the ceiling, some ran under the edges of the windowsill, and some boxes were big enough to be awkward to carry, sort of like her new printer. The various sizes and heights were stairsteps to Patch, who flew around the room, leaping and climbing and generally having a wonderful time.

"Can't you at least try to be good?" she chastised him. "You're going to blow it."

He climbed to the top of the tallest stack and lay down, his paws crossed casually in front of him. He blinked at her as if to say, "What are you talking about?"

She glared back. "Come on, you little devil. Get down here."

She approached him carefully. She expected him to leap over her and escape, but he allowed her to reach up and snag him. When she pulled him close, he began to purr.

"You are incorrigible."

He answered by snuggling closer and purring harder.

Ashley was about to leave the room when the label on the closest box caught her eye. It showed a picture of a bowl. Granted it was a black-and-white image, but Ashley had seen that bowl recently at Eagle's Nest Gifts. She studied the other boxes and recognized a couple of vases that had also been at the gift shop. Unease knotting her insides, she searched until she found the label she was afraid she would. The picture of a little turtle with an exaggerated hump of a shell was glued to several of the smaller boxes.

Absently petting the temporarily cooperative Patch, Ashley let herself out of the room. A whole room of Navajo pottery struck her as rather odd. Had Bette bought all these pieces with her own money—or corporate funds? Was she taking MarleyHolmes's support of Margaret White Bear's artisan enclave to a questionable extreme?

19

With Patch tucked firmly under her arm, Ashley made her way back to the kitchen. She was tempted to put Patch in his carrier and go back to fix the bedroom he'd left in disarray, but Bette needed to know what she'd be getting into if she decided to keep Patch, so she might as well let him scamper around a bit more.

Just before they entered the kitchen, Ashley wrapped her hands around Patch's middle and brought him face to face with her. He hung passively, for all the world the most docile cat alive. "Your future is on the line," she whispered.

He blinked his pumpkin eyes.

She set him on the floor. He immediately jumped onto a stool.

Bette nodded approval. "I wouldn't want to be on the floor either."

"He's a climber," Ashley said, and Patch cut his eyes at her as if asking why she was giving away his secrets. "And his tail's a weapon all its own."

He jumped onto the island and walked to the white bowl filled with green apples. He rubbed his head against it. Bette thought he was scratching his head, but Ashley suspected he was testing its weight. He sat beside it as if in thought. Would he butt it over the edge with his head or "accidentally" knock it over with his tail? Ashley held her breath.

Bette had turned the coffee cake onto a brilliant blue plate with yellow scallops all around the edges. It looked nothing like the Navajo pottery in the storage room, which made Ashley even more curious. The native pieces didn't seem to be Bette's style, so why did she have so many of them? Gifts, she supposed. Christmas was coming up, after all, and perhaps she'd bought one item for everyone on her list.

While Ashley's thoughts meandered, Patch jumped effortlessly from the island to the counter, where he began to stalk the cake. Apparently the apples weren't as tempting as the scent of fresh baked goods.

"Not for you, my boy." Bette lifted the plate and brought it to the table. Patch walked to the end of the counter and eyed the cake, now several feet away. Ashley bit back a smile at his expression. He was debating a jump or two—she just knew it.

Bette opened a cupboard, pulled out a pair of colorful mugs, and put them on the counter by the coffee machine. "Why don't you cut the cake while I pour the coffee, Ashley?" She grabbed a spatula with a serrated edge and handed it over.

"Sure." Ashley went to the table, where she cut and plated two pieces with the spatula, then sat in one of the chairs.

"How do you take your coffee?" Bette glanced over her shoulder at Ashley.

Ashley gave her order as Patch jumped to the floor with a soft thud. He walked to the island and rubbed the side of his face against one sharp corner of the base. She watched him curiously. Was he merely scratching an itch, plotting another tour of exploration, or planning his assault on the coffee cake?

Bette came to the table with the coffee mugs in her hands. "Here you go."

Ashley pulled the mug toward her. The coffee smelled delicious. She picked up her spoon and slowly stirred the liquid, savoring the twin fragrances of coffee and baked goods.

Without warning, Patch jumped up to the table, landing beside Ashley's right hand. A couple more inches and he'd have been in her coffee mug.

Bette eyed him with less warmth than a few minutes ago. "You said he was a jumper. I guess I never thought that meant the table."

"I'm afraid the purpose of a surface doesn't interest him. He only cares about the jump to it."

"Well, down, kitty." Bette fluttered her hands in his direction. He, of course, did not move.

Ashley left her spoon in the mug and grabbed Patch under the belly. With one swift move, she set him on the floor. "Stay," she ordered, assuming he wouldn't. She set her napkin in her lap, picked up her fork, and scooped up a bite of coffee cake. The cinnamon and brown sugar melted on her tongue. "This is delicious, Bette."

Ashley reached for her mug to wash down the cake, but all of a sudden Patch was beside her again. Bette barely concealed a hiss of displeasure.

"I'll put him in his carrier." Ashley stood.

Patch sensed her intent and jumped, not to the floor but toward the middle of the table. In the process, he bumped hard against her mug, knocking it over. The contents flowed in a tidal wave directly at Bette, who issued an exclamation of dismay.

Ashley grabbed him before he got coffee all over himself and walked it all over the kitchen. She loaded him into his carrier, which still sat on the counter, and zipped him in, knowing beyond doubt that Patch and Bette were not a match made in heaven or anywhere else. She needed to get him out of here as quickly as possible.

At the table, Bette mopped frantically at the spill with a fistful of paper towels. Brown liquid spattered her designer jeans. Ashley grabbed the few remaining towels on the spindle and went to help. There was a chill in Bette's eyes.

"Really, Ashley. You think that animal is suitable for adoption?" The way she said *animal* made Patch sound like a cockroach instead of an overactive kitten.

Ashley caught a trickle of coffee as it was about to fall to the floor. "I think he's fine for someone to adopt, but maybe not right for you." She forced a laugh. "You have far too many lovely things for an active pet like Patch. Maybe an older cat, or a small dog who is already trained."

"I'm rethinking my whole plan." Bette opened the door beneath her sink and dropped the wet paper towels in the wastebasket hidden there. She pulled out a new roll. "I'm probably better off without a pet." She shut the door with more force than necessary.

Suddenly eager to leave, Ashley hurriedly stuffed her own paper towel into her pocket and reached for the carrier full of mischievous kitten. "We'll get out of your hair, Bette. Thanks so much for the invitation. The coffee cake was delicious." She saw it sitting in a puddle of coffee. "And thanks for considering Patch."

Bette led the way to the front hall. She gave Ashley her coat and had the door open before Ashley had time to zip up. She grabbed Patch and left.

Ashley had barely driven a block before she had to pull over so she could laugh. "Oh, Patch. If she's upset with us now, wait until she sees your trail of destruction in the bedroom wing." She wiped her eyes. "At least I don't have to wonder if I should ever say anything to her about her boyfriend. I'm pretty sure there will be no more cozy lunches at Miss Abigale's with her."

As she got back on the road, she wondered whether she'd pulled the door to the storage room closed or not. With a shrug, she figured it was one more strike against her and Patch.

Seeing that Patch had started snoozing in the carrier, Ashley drove out to Marley Meadows. With most adults at work and kids at school, the activity level at the ranch was significantly less than on the weekend. She parked next to the barn.

She'd thought a lot about Skye since she'd seen her Sunday. Obviously the ranch where she had been bred had done no separation training before selling her. The present owner, while doing her best for Skye, also didn't understand the ingrained herd instinct of horses.

Since it was too late for separation preparation or prevention, the situation called for correction. Skye saw herself as alone with no leader to watch over her, no friends to protect her. It was her against the world.

Ashley walked into the barn thinking about the plan she and Lowell might devise for Skye. Surely he'd given the horse a lot of thought too and would have several suggestions.

"Geez, don't you ever do anything right?"

Ashley recognized Rani's voice.

There was the rumble of a male responding, but his words weren't clear. They were in a stall down the row, and Ashley was blocked from their view. They didn't know their argument was being overheard.

"Well, I think the gap year was a mistake." Rani was apparently tearing into Garrett again. After another grumbled response, she snapped, "Don't give me that. You almost killed Sweetie, and it's your fault Mark messed up his ankle. If you'd done your job—"

Ashley couldn't hear much of the reply, but the word "sorry" slipped out as well as "not my job."

"Of course it was your job, and you wouldn't recognize 'sorry' if it punched you in the nose." Rani's voice rose as her anger heightened. "You're an idiot!"

Ashley decided to pretend she'd just arrived. "Lowell?" she called. "Are you in here?"

Rani peered around a stall door. "Hi, Dr. Hart." Now she was all smiles and charm.

"Hi, Rani. I'm here to check on Skye."

Rani waved her hand toward the open barn door at the end of the row of stalls. "She's out there somewhere."

"By herself?" Surely Lowell knew not to leave her alone. She was in such distress that she might inadvertently hurt herself.

A clatter of hooves drew Ashley's attention behind her. Garrett walked into the barn with Skye following him on a relaxed lead.

"Hi, Dr. Hart. Are you here to see Skye?" He smiled over his shoulder at the horse. "Our girl's doing well. Aren't you, pretty lady?"

Skye nickered.

"When you're with her." Rani walked toward her brother. "Or when Molly's around. Skye likes Molly."

"Molly's big and calm," Garrett said.

"You wouldn't believe how great Garrett's been with her, Dr. Hart." Rani smiled proudly at her brother. "I keep telling him horses are his thing, not dogs."

Wait a minute. Rani was praising Garrett? Ashley peered down the row. Who was in the stall?

Garrett stopped walking, and Skye stopped a few feet behind. He grinned at the horse. "Good girl. We've been working on that," he explained to Ashley, with no small amount of pride in his voice.

Not able to decide which was more surprising—Rani's attitude or Skye's demeanor—Ashley glanced from the boy to the horse who stood calmly behind him. He'd established himself as her leader in a little over forty-eight hours. Amazing.

"At least *someone* takes his responsibility seriously." Rani pitched her voice to be heard in the stall she'd exited.

"I take responsibility," came whirling back.

"When you feel like it." Scorn bristled in Rani's tone.

"It's worked out for me so far." Henry emerged from the stall pushing a wheelbarrow full of used straw. He tossed his head to get his too-long hair out of his face.

"Is the stall ready for her?" Garrett asked.

"Needs clean straw," Henry answered. "Let me get rid of this, and I'll get it."

"You're actually going to do your job?" Rani glared at him.

Henry winked at her.

She muttered, "Idiot," under her breath and stalked out of the barn.

Henry watched her go with a sweet smile. "I love that girl. She doesn't know it yet, but I'm going to marry her."

Garrett snorted. "Do yourself a favor and don't."

Henry grinned and disappeared with his wheelbarrow.

"I've got a question I must ask." Ashley moved toward Skye, who took a step backward, tightening her lead. Ashley stopped immediately.

"Just a second." Garrett led the mare from the barn, walked a large circle, and reentered, the lead again relaxed. "Ask away."

"I heard Rani tell Henry he was responsible for Sweetie getting sick. The day she did get sick, Rani accused you of being responsible." Ashley shook her head, confused. "I don't get it."

"She was mad at me because I talked Mom and Mark into hiring Henry in spite of his lack of experience," Garrett said. "He hadn't taken the trash out, and in her mind, that was my fault because I got him the job."

"I guess that makes sense in a roundabout way."

Garrett smirked. "In a Rani way."

"So, tell me about Skye."

Garrett's face lit up. "She was in the pasture with the other horses for a little while."

"That must have been interesting. How did she do?"

"She was wary of them. Spent most of her time backed into a corner, keeping one eye on them and the other on me. As long as she could see me, she didn't act out, but she didn't mingle."

"They might have four legs, but they're strangers."

"She'll get used to them. I give her carrots whenever I put her with them. She'll start to associate a treat with them, and then she'll start to like them."

Ashley studied this young man who had shown an understanding of how horses think that many ranchers never got. "Are you going to be her primary caregiver?"

"I asked Lowell if I could be, and he said yes." He walked Skye toward her stall, and she immediately became agitated, pulling back on her lead. When Garrett walked on past, she calmed and followed. He walked back and forth past the stall several times without making any effort to enter, and each time, her distress lessened. "Good girl, Skye," he murmured.

His patience was amazing, and his skill with the horse was extraordinary. As he walked Skye, he talked to Ashley.

"When she found herself alone in that stall Saturday night, it was dark and silent and very scary for her. She was missing her herd, and she didn't recognize anything. No wonder she went slightly nuts. I need to get her to accept the stall as an unthreatening place, a sanctuary rather than a prison. She needs to enter it willingly. Given the increasing cold and short days of winter, she can only be outside a limited amount of time, like the other horses. She has to learn to feel safe in the stall."

"She's making you her herd, you know," Ashley said gently. "That will create another problem when it's time for her to go back to her owner."

He nodded. "I know. But first things first. I want to get her at ease with being here at the ranch, being in her stall. Then we can deal with teaching her to live without me."

"How will you do that?" Ashley was finding this new version of Garrett fascinating.

"I remember my father dealing with an anxious horse who couldn't stand being away from her best buddy. He began by separating them by distance, a little more each day. They could still see each other, but they weren't in the same paddock or space. Then he began working the anxious horse when she went near her buddy. Not every time, of course, but some time each day. He'd make her walk in circles. He'd saddle her and ride her. She learned that if she got near her buddy, there was a good chance she'd have to work. She wasn't so anxious to be near her buddy anymore." He scratched Skye under the chin. "I thought I'd eventually try the same thing, with one of the ranch hands working her when she came near me."

"As long as you don't use me." Henry joined them.

Garrett laughed. "You don't have to worry about that."

Henry nodded toward Garrett. "He is amazing with her, Dr. Hart. Even I'm impressed, and I don't impress easily."

Garrett appeared pleased at the compliment. "You didn't do too badly yourself, especially given your lack of experience with horses."

Rani walked back in the barn and heard the last comment. "Henry doesn't know anything about horses."

"Too true." Henry shuddered. "All those big teeth and that huge body. She outweighs me by a scary amount. She could crush me if she wanted."

"If she wanted." Rani rounded on Garrett. "You're not letting him near Skye, are you?"

Garrett gave her a look. "Who do you think stepped in for me during the night while you were tucked up all cozy in your bed?"

"You let Henry keep Skye company?" Rani yelped. "By himself?"

"With help from Molly and Sonny and Claudette." Garrett pointed to a black-and-white cat who stalked back and forth on the stall's half door. "Skye likes the animals. She probably had some as barn mates where she was raised. She wasn't happy when I left her, but if she could see Henry and the animals, she didn't thrash around."

"Claudette's the best." Henry walked to the cat and picked her up. He draped her around his neck like a furry scarf. She lay there, limp and content.

Rani stared. "How did you do that? She doesn't let anyone touch her."

Henry smirked. "Some of us are horse whisperers. Some of us are cat whisperers."

Inspiration struck Ashley. "Henry, will you go out to my car and get the carrier on the back seat?" She held out the keys.

Henry seemed surprised, but he put Claudette down and took the keys. "Be right back."

Claudette disappeared into the tack room.

Garrett watched his friend go. "He's a computer genius, our Henry. His IQ is off the charts."

"Not good for anything but computers." Rani's razor-sharp tongue cut as usual.

Garrett frowned at his sister. "Have you ever listened to yourself? It's a miracle you have any friends."

Hurt showed in her eyes. "I have lots of friends."

"Well, ease up on Henry," Garrett said. "He's my friend." When Rani made a sound of disgust, Garrett suddenly became inches taller and broader as he glared down at her. "I mean it."

She ducked her head and held up her hand. "Okay, okay."

Henry returned, the carrier hanging from one hand and Patch cuddled in the other. Both boy and cat seemed smitten.

"You like him?" Ashley knew a silly question when she asked it. "Though I think you've met before."

"We have?" He shook his head. "I don't think so."

"Last Sunday. On my front steps."

Color stained Henry's cheeks. "Oh."

"I spent the last few days blaming Garrett," Ashley said.

"Oops." Henry seemed to find that funny.

"For what?" Garrett asked.

"Leaving the kittens at her house." Henry shrugged. "I tried taking them to the rescue your mom sent me to, but they had a sign up that they were closed for an emergency. I used my phone to find Dr. Hart's address. I knew a vet would take good care of them."

Garrett shook his head. "That was a gamble."

"I got the kittens cared for, didn't I?" the other boy replied.

"You are the worst." Rani's venom was flowing in spite of her brother's scolding. "And how'd you know she'd find them?"

Henry rolled his eyes. "I knew she was home." He held Patch up for all to see. "He's fine." He scratched Patch behind his ears, and the kitten soaked it up.

As she listened to the kids talk, Ashley thought back over the conversations she'd heard between Kristin and Mark about an irresponsible boy. They hadn't been talking about Garrett. They'd been talking about Henry, doing their best to make a responsible young man out of him. Well, she was going to do her part.

She raised an eyebrow in question to Garrett. He understood and nodded.

"Would you like Patch, Henry?" Ashley asked. "He's looking for his human."

Henry froze, wonder on his face. "He could be mine?" He shook his hair from his eyes. "I always wanted a pet, but my mom's allergic."

"But you live here now, right? He's yours if you promise to feed him and clean his litter box." Ashley didn't bother to add "and love him." It was obvious the boy already did that.

Henry studied Patch, who leaned back in the boy's grip and returned the stare. "I think he'll remind me if I forget any of it—not that I ever would." He added the last bit as he saw Rani shake her head as if disbelieving his ability to handle something so basic.

"I'll give you a list of the things you'll need to buy for him," Ashley said. "Be aware that he's very active and loves to climb."

"This place will be great for him." Henry set Patch on the floor, and the kitten immediately leaped atop a stall door.

"You need to establish yourself as his owner," Ashley said. "Feed him regularly so he doesn't turn into a barn mouser. Make sure he sleeps in your room."

"Every night." Henry walked to Patch, who watched him approach without running. Henry picked him up and draped him around his neck. Patch lay there, eyes closed. Henry gently cupped the animal's lolling head.

Satisfaction rolled through Ashley. "Do you come from a large family, Henry?"

"There are seven of us kids," he answered. "I'm the youngest."

Garrett had been walking Skye and stopped in front of her stall. She stared at it, her eyes wide. She began pawing the ground with her right front foot, a sign of agitation. Immediately, he began to walk again. Skye followed with a brief shake of her head.

Henry leaned one shoulder against the barn wall and watched, arms across his chest and feet crossed at the ankles, Patch still draped around his neck. The pose made him appear older and more confident. Ashley caught a glimpse of the man he might become.

"So you're learning to be a ranch hand?" she asked.

Henry made a face. "Only for this year. I'm trying to put a little money in the bank before college."

Garrett grinned at his friend. "I talked Mom and Mark into offering him a place to live and earn during his gap year so he'll be able to do school without the pressure of covering his living expenses. He's got an all-expenses-paid education waiting for him."

Henry gave a self-conscious smile. "Computers are my passion. I'm not sure where I'll land yet job wise—the opportunities in the field are endless—but I'll get at least one PhD. That I know."

Rani rolled her eyes. "A bit full of yourself, aren't you?"

Henry shrugged. "Truth is truth, whether you like it or not." He straightened. "All I can say is it's a good thing the rest of your family is nicer to me than you are."

Rani rolled her eyes again.

Garrett led Skye to the stall door but didn't try to take her in. She eyed it nervously, though she didn't paw the ground this time. He picked up a brush and began grooming her. "I think maybe the soothing motion of the brush will calm her agitation at being here."

"Good thinking," Ashley said.

"He needs to go to college for horses," Henry said.

"That's equine studies or equine management, genius." Rani's tone was wry, though Ashley thought there was less acid in it than usual.

"Which is basically what I said," Henry responded stubbornly.

Rani offered him one last glare, then shifted her attention to Ashley. "I came back, Dr. Hart, because I was wondering if I could feature Max on my show."

Ashley laughed in surprise, but readily agreed. "He'd love it. How would you dress him?"

"I haven't figured it all out yet, but his costume will have something to do with the breed's history," Rani said, her eyes bright with excitement. "Dalmatians are firehouse dogs, obviously. But they also rode with carriage drivers back in the day to help protect the horses from wild dogs and other dangerous animals. Their presence actually has a notable calming effect on horses."

"I'm sure whatever you come up with will be wonderful," Ashley said, eager to find out what that might be. "Thank you for thinking of us."

Rani smiled. "You bet."

Garrett leaned toward his sister. "See what being nice to people feels like?"

Thunderclouds reappeared immediately in Rani's eyes.

Before an argument began in earnest, Ashley asked Henry, "Where did you grow up, Henry? Not on a ranch, I take it."

"My parents have a small plot of land not too far out of town that backs up to White River National Forest," Henry answered. "As far as my dad's concerned, he owns the whole forest and is free to hunt and wander at will. He's former military and prefers a more rustic approach to living, so we don't even have a TV. My mom sort of goes along with it, keeping the rest of us together the best she can." He tossed his hair out of his eyes again and added quietly, "Dad's generally a nice guy, but he suffers from mental issues." He made a wry face. "He's a genius too."

Ashley's heart went out to the boy, who obviously worried about genetics.

"He came back from a deployment like this," Henry said, answering her unspoken question. "A head injury caused by a roadside bomb. Mom stayed with him, and they managed to raise all seven of us. Everyone has moved out now, most of the older ones being in the military. The lack of kid chaos will be good for him."

"I hope so," Ashley said. "So if you grew up without a TV, how did you wind up a computer geek?"

"Lots of quality time in the school computer lab," Henry said.

"He's the one who helped Rani and me get everything set up for our shows," Garrett said. "Without him, we'd still be using our phones."

"No big deal." Henry pointed his index finger at Garrett. "I knew you invited me to your place that first time because you wanted to use me."

"It certainly wasn't because he liked you," Rani said, though her eyes twinkled with teasing. "You were the class weirdo."

"I was." Henry shrugged. "Used to bother me, but not so much anymore. I am what I am."

"Whatever that is." Rani rolled her eyes, and Henry grinned at her.

"Are you the one who set up the livestream on Sweetie and her pups?" Ashley asked him.

"I sure am," Henry said.

Rani threw him another of her mocking glances. "You can do all kinds of complex technology stuff, but you can't remember to take out the trash."

"I've got important things on my mind," Henry protested.

Ashley looked from Henry to Garrett. "Does the streaming footage get saved somewhere?"

Henry got it immediately. "You want to check what happened when Sweetie got sick."

Ashley shook her head solemnly. "I want to check on something even more serious—what happened when a man who's now dead came for brunch."

20

Garrett didn't get it at first. "You think Mark took Ed Warner to see the puppies?"

"Who knows?" Ashley wouldn't be surprised though. Mark loved Sweetie and her puppies. "He took him to see the horses."

Garrett blinked. "How do you know?"

"Mr. Ridley told me," Ashley said. "Mr. Warner was thinking of boarding a horse here."

Henry shook his head in exasperation. "I keep telling you, Garrett. Mark loves the ranch." When Garrett gave a skeptical growl, Henry added, "And he loves your mom. Anybody can see that."

Ashley nodded. "I agree."

Henry's expression became sympathetic. "You're allowed to like Mark, Garrett. It doesn't make you unfaithful to your father's memory. I love Claudette, but that doesn't mean I can't like Patch too."

Not the best metaphor, but it was very Henry.

Garrett dug in his heels. "You never knew my dad."

"Which I'm sorry about," Henry said. "From what everyone says, he was a great man. But Mark's a great guy too, in his own way."

Rani spoke up. "Mom's happy, Garrett. Isn't that what counts?"

Garrett frowned at his sister. "Of course you'd take his side about this."

She pulled a face at that. "It took me a while, but I think Mark's okay. And Mom's happier than she's been since Dad died."

Henry nudged Garrett with his elbow. "You don't have to pick one or the other. It can be both."

Ashley recognized a much-discussed topic when she heard one. Garrett had to resolve his conflicts on his own. She thought he might appreciate a reprieve from this topic of conversation. "So, can we access that footage?" she asked.

Garrett's tight shoulders sagged with relief at the change of subject. "Yes, but why?"

"I'm thinking if Mr. Warner and Mark visited the dogs or even just went out through the back door, the cameras might have caught something." Ashley shrugged. "It's worth checking."

"Maybe the cameras caught someone skulking." Rani's eyes glowed as she got caught up in the possibilities.

Garrett crossed his arms over his chest. "Oh, come on. You really think our livestream caught a murderer?"

"Why not?" Rani glared at him, hands on hips.

"You know what I think?" Henry shook the hair from his eyes again.

"You think you'll finally get a haircut?" Rani jabbed.

Henry ignored her. "I think Mr. Holmes should have hired me instead of that poor guy. I'd have found the leak."

"And told him how to fix it, I suppose?" Rani scowled.

Henry nodded. "Probably."

"Then you'd be dead instead of him." And she stormed out.

Henry grinned after her. "I didn't know she cared."

A few minutes later, Garrett got Skye in her stall with minimal fuss, and then he and Henry disappeared to check the tape. Marveling at Garrett's surprising gift, Ashley examined the horse, glad to see Skye was very healthy except for her anxiety, which at the moment was on low boil. Once she had wrapped with Skye, Ashley texted Kristin to ask if she could check the puppies and Sweetie while she was here.

Kristin met her at the back door with a little scrap of mewling fur in her hands. "I call this one Alice."

"Because she lives in a wonderland." Ashley swung her arm to indicate Marley Meadows.

Kristin laughed. "Something like that. Mr. Ridley is here, and I'm showing him the puppies. Come on in."

Kristin led the way to the whelping room, setting Alice back in the enclosure once inside. Ashley followed, noting the cameras as she entered. Their directions of focus meant only one could have recorded something useful. The one that was aimed directly down on the dogs was too limited, but the one that had a wide view of the room might have caught a clue.

It was a long shot at best, but one they'd be foolish to ignore.

As Ashley and Oliver were exchanging greetings, a bell sounded in another room.

Kristin started for the door. "It's Mark in the living room, wondering where we are. He's on the sofa and is cranky because he hurts and isn't as mobile as he wants to be, and he's alone while we're off having fun."

"Go back to him." Ashley knelt beside the box. "I'll check on these guys and meet up with you in a little bit."

Kristin and the investigator left, and Ashley had a fun few minutes cuddling and examining the fast-growing pups. She weighed and measured and listened to hearts, especially Sweetie's, to make certain there were no repercussions from her illness. When she was finished, she disposed of her refuse in the container by the door, which she noted was almost empty. Henry had learned his lesson.

As she picked up her medical bag, Garrett, Henry, and Rani spilled into the room, faces alight with excitement.

"We checked," Henry announced. Patch was tucked under his arm.

"And we saw something." Rani was too thrilled to be grumpy.

"We saw hands." Garrett was beside himself with excitement. "They untied the closed bag—"

"See?" Henry interrupted. "I told you I closed it. I may have forgotten to take it out, but I closed it. It was secured from the dogs." He was delighted with this confirmation that he wasn't completely at fault. He bent over Sweetie and patted her head. "Now you know I'm not the bad guy." She licked his hand. Patch eyed her and put a paw on her head. She pushed gently back, and they seemed to find a common peace.

"You still left the bag lying there," Rani said. "For days."

Garrett waved a hand to stop the arguing, then picked up the story. "On the footage, you can see a hand put a to-go cup in the bag, tucking it in carefully so it wouldn't fall out, but not taking time to retie the bag again."

"Like the person was in a hurry." Henry bounced on his toes with excitement.

"Like they might get caught." Rani's eyes shone.

"A man's hands or a woman's?" Ashley asked.

Their unbridled enthusiasm came to a screeching halt.

"I'm not sure. It's too dim out there." Rani pointed to the hall.

"The video isn't all that clear," Henry admitted. "Want me to send it to you? Maybe you'll see something we didn't."

"Yes, I'd love to see it." Ashley gave him her phone number and e-mail address, which he noted on his phone.

"I'll e-mail it over and you can watch it on your phone, but it'll be small," Henry told her. "You can watch the video on your computer later to see if you can spot a clue." He appeared slightly dazed. "I just said the word 'clue' in real life."

Ashley smiled at the three kids. "You may have found the method of the murder. You need to give this video to Chief Maloney immediately. Why don't I call and let him know to expect it?"

The teens exchanged glances, vibrating with tension and importance.

They were part of a murder investigation without facing any of the danger often associated with one. It didn't get much better than that.

"I can put it on a flash drive for him." Henry started from the room. "I'll drive."

"You will not." Rani grabbed the back of his shirt. "Garrett will drive. I trust him."

As the three left, Henry beamed at Ashley. "She really likes me."

While Ashley called the local police number, she wondered about geniuses and social cues. She would be interested to see what Henry and Rani's dynamic was in about five years. Lanky Henry would fill out a bit and smooth off some of his rough edges, maybe even get a haircut. He'd be well into his PhD studies, his mind sharp, his wit equally so. Rani would mature and learn to curb her tongue—hopefully. If anything, she'd be even more beautiful and even richer from Dog Duds.

Would they be as good a match as Henry hoped? *Stranger things have happened,* Ashley thought. *Look at Clint and Helen or Kristin and Mark.*

Angie Sherman answered, and Ashley explained about the kids coming her way. "I don't know if what they've found will help, but it certainly needs to be checked out."

"I'll tell the chief, and he'll be waiting," Angie assured her.

Feeling hopeful, Ashley walked to the living room. Mark lay on the sofa while Oliver paced restlessly around the room, examining framed photographs and knickknacks.

Mark gestured for her to take a seat. "Kristin's getting some coffee. You want a cup?"

"No thank you." Ashley smiled her appreciation but remained standing, planning on leaving as soon as she gave her Sweetie report to Kristin. "How are you feeling?"

Mark glared at his leg, resting on pillows. His cast was royal blue. Ashley laughed. "Enough said."

Kristin walked in with a tray holding a coffee carafe and cups as well as a can of ginger ale and a glass of ice. She poured the ginger ale for Mark. "Coffee still tastes strange to him after the anesthesia."

"I can talk for myself," Mark groused as he took the glass. "Ashley, coffee tastes weird since they put me under."

Kristin gave him her stern face. "You want to know how he's feeling, Ashley? He's feeling sorry for himself, but he won't take pain meds. He doesn't want to 'cloud his thinking.'" She made air quotes, balancing her words on the delicate edge between sympathy and mockery. She bent and kissed his forehead. "Old bear."

Mark caught her hand and squeezed.

Oliver stopped at a shelf that held decorative items—a framed picture of Garrett and Rani as small children, a beautifully detailed china King Charles spaniel, a pair of silver-prize vases with Sweetie's full name and the event engraved, and a Navajo bowl in terra-cotta, aqua, and cream featuring a beautiful circular pattern.

He examined the vases, carefully reading the inscriptions. "Impressive."

Kristin smiled. "I'm sorry you never got to see her in action."

Oliver gestured to the bowl. "Pretty."

"Mark gave it to me a couple of weeks ago to celebrate the anniversary of our first date. It's a signed original, done by a Navajo artisan that MarleyHolmes sponsors." Pleasure saturated Kristin's voice.

The investigator shook his head. "I hate to tell you, but it's a fake."

"What?" Mark pushed himself to sit straighter. "It's signed."

Ashley had a sinking feeling about her own little turtle, especially as she thought of all the boxes in that spare room at Bette's. "Did you get it at Eagle's Nest Gifts, Mark?"

He nodded. "I figured buying it from Marylouise would support both her and Margaret White Bear. How did you know?"

"I bought myself a Navajo turtle there. Then I went back the next day and bought one in a different color for Holly's birthday. Both the turtles are signed by Margaret White Bear too." Ashley fought the feeling she'd been taken in. "I researched the artisan enclave online after I bought the piece. Their website lists at least twenty different artists with photos of their work and their studio."

"I'm not surprised," Oliver said. "That's a sign of a very sophisticated ring."

"But the piece is so beautiful." Kristin was crestfallen.

"I agree. Enjoy it that way, not as a one of a kind." Oliver set it carefully back on the shelf. "If they wanted to sell it as Navajo-style pottery, they'd be fine. If they didn't claim it was an original, they'd be fine. Of course, they couldn't sell it for nearly as much money."

"I was surprised the turtle wasn't more expensive," Ashley said.

Mark gave a soft snort, which made Ashley think his piece had been pretty pricey. "It's probably made in a factory somewhere by people who are anything but Native American." His tone was sour.

"Probably," Oliver agreed.

Ashley went to the shelf and picked up the bowl. She flipped it over and stared at the signature, which appeared to be the same as the one on the bottom of her turtle. "Is there even a Margaret White Bear?"

Oliver shook his head. "I doubt it. At least not one who's a pottery artist. RBI has done a couple of investigations into fake Native American art. It's big business. The mass-produced items in this particular scam are very well done."

Ashley winced as she thought of Bette again, and of Marylouise at Eagle's Nest Gifts. *Wait until they learn they've been scammed.*

Oliver took a chair and reached for the coffee Kristin had poured for him. "I'll clue in the police on what I know about the fake art. They can shut down the local outlet and try to trace the supply chain. This stuff is floating around all over the West."

"Coffee, Ashley?" Kristin held up the carafe.

Ashley checked her watch, second-guessing her earlier refusal of a cup. She had plenty of time before office hours this afternoon, and as long as no emergency calls came in, she'd enjoy the conversation, especially since she might learn more about Margaret White Bear and counterfeit art.

Her phone dinged with an incoming message. Henry had sent her the video from the livestream. She opened the file.

The short video caught a sliver of the hall. At this resolution, she could just make out the garbage bag and hands, but that was about it. The room with the puppies was bright and clear, but the small section of hall visible through the room's door was dim and unfocused.

Despite the darkness, Ashley saw hands quickly untying the trash bag. They stuffed a to-go cup inside but didn't take time to resecure the garbage bag ties. Then the hands were gone. She watched again, stopping the video and enlarging the hands. Everything became grainier. She studied the hands, hoping for an identifying mark like a ring, a tattoo, or a scar. Wouldn't that be convenient?

"Oliver, you'll want to see this." She passed her phone to the investigator.

He watched the short video with a confused look. "Someone put a cup in the trash. I don't get it."

"That video is from the day Ed Warner was killed," Ashley said. "The bag holds the trash that made Sweetie ill."

Oliver blinked. "You think it was that cup?"

"Maybe."

"Let me see." Mark held out a hand.

Oliver passed the phone over, and Mark watched with Kristin peering over his shoulder.

Ashley sank into the chair Mark had offered her earlier. "The kids are on their way to the police station to show Chief Maloney."

"And I thought the livestream was a silly idea." Mark relaxed back against the pillows. "I need to apologize to Garrett."

Kristin took the phone and watched again. She used her index finger and thumb to enlarge the picture. She made a choking sound.

"What's wrong?" Mark asked, all concern.

Kristin stared at the phone, her expression a combination of disbelief and despair. "I know whose hands those are."

21

Kristin's finger shook as she pointed. "See?"

Mark studied the picture, then drew in a sharp breath. "I'm so sorry. I hoped that wouldn't be the case." He reached for her.

Kristin frowned and pulled back. "What do you mean, you hoped it wouldn't be the case?"

He waved a hand. "Later."

"What did you see?" Ashley had studied the image plenty and hadn't noticed anything she would expect to wound Kristin so clearly.

Oliver grabbed the phone. "What am I looking for?"

Kristin drew in a shaky breath. "The bandage on her wrist."

There'd been a bandage? Ashley had been so busy searching for a clue, she'd missed it.

"Why is that worth noting?" Oliver's dark brows formed a V over his nose.

"It belongs to Bette DeVane." As if saying those words had sapped her of all energy, Kristin sank onto the edge of a chair. "It was right after her carpal tunnel surgery, and we had all been impressed by the minimal bandage on the inside of her wrist. They used to wrap you in miles of gauze." She put a hand over her mouth as if to stifle a cry. The sorrowful expression on her face tore at Ashley's heart.

"So she was here that Sunday for your brunch with Ed Warner?" Ashley considered what that new piece of information might mean.

Kristin shook her head. "She showed up while Ed and Mark were walking and talking. She said she felt like dropping by. I never thought anything about it because she's been doing that since forever." Kristin's voice caught. "We're best friends."

Mark patted the cushion beside him on the couch. "Come here, Kris."

She moved to sit beside him, leaning into him as tears spilled down her face.

"Let me get this straight." Oliver pointed at the video and the bandage, which Ashley could make out now that her eyes had adapted to the video. "This person killed Ed Warner?"

Mark ran his hand up and down Kristin's back. "She at least tried to hide the cup that later made Sweetie sick, but yes, I think so."

"So she came because she knew he was here," Oliver said.

Mark glanced at Kristin. "Did she know he was here?"

"I don't think so. I certainly didn't tell her. There was no reason I should." Kristin frowned from Ashley to Oliver. "As far as I was concerned, he was a business contact of Mark's who came to brunch. I didn't know there was anything clandestine going on. Mark didn't tell me." There was a little bit of snip in the last words.

"Because I wanted to be wrong." Mark held her hand. "If she'd proved to be innocent, you'd never think less of her."

"So she was one of the people Ed was investigating?" Her voice was sad.

"Along with Chaz Romaine. As head of IT, he was in charge of the development team, and she was in charge of rolling out the new product. They were the only two besides me who had the entire package available to them. Others merely knew their parts of the puzzle."

"But she didn't know she was being investigated?" Oliver asked.

"She did not," Mark said firmly.

"She didn't expect to see Ed here," Oliver surmised.

Mark shook his head. "She expected Kristin and me, so she brought three coffees. Kris went to the kitchen and got another for herself."

Oliver shook his head. "She just happened to have poison conveniently on her person when she came to visit and managed to unobtrusively get it into the lidded to-go cup she gave Ed?"

"Well, she must have had the tetrodotoxin with her," Ashley said. "We know that because she used it. And she tried to hide the evidence by putting the cup in the trash ready to go out the door." She turned to Kristin. "Speaking of which, I think I figured out what happened with Sweetie."

Kristin lifted her tearstained face. "What?"

"I think she was rooting through the trash, drawn by the scent of the candy wrappers," Ashley explained. "She came to the to-go cup, got a touch of residue on her nose, and licked at it to clear away the scent."

"That fits," Mark said. "She's always disliked coffee."

"The barest suggestion of the poison." Kristin nodded. "But Bette? Her godmother? She put Sweetie in such danger."

"She had no idea Sweetie would get anywhere near that cup," Ashley pointed out. "At least she's innocent of that, anyway."

"I'm still hung up on why she had the poison with her if she didn't know about Ed." Oliver started pacing. "Tell me about their interactions."

Mark shifted on the couch. "As I remember it, when he and I walked into the house and the dining room, I was saying how I wanted him to continue his investigation. That's where we met Bette, who seemed genuinely surprised. A few questions about who he was and what he was investigating, and Bette figured it out. We tried to dodge, but Bette is not easily sidetracked. She was not happy. In fact, she's barely spoken to me since."

Ashley recalled the subtle—and not-so-subtle—digs Bette had made at Mark during their conversations. Today's revelations certainly shed light on the reasoning behind that.

Mark took Kristin's hand. "Remember how insistent she was that Ed take that specific coffee? 'It's a Mountain Goat special. You'll love it.'" Mark went quiet for a moment. "It's the one I usually get."

"Ah," Oliver said softly as if things suddenly made sense.

Kristin paled. "No. She wouldn't!"

Mark appeared shaken at the thought that he might have been the intended victim. "She must have guessed that I suspected her even before she met Ed here. I guess I wasn't as clever as I thought."

"Or," Oliver said, "she wanted you out of the way. Vice presidents sometimes go to extremes to become presidents."

Ashley looked away from Mark's stricken face and Kristin's distress. Her eyes fell on a pile of business magazines on the coffee table, obviously there for Mark. Her breath caught. "Who's that?"

"Who?" Mark asked distractedly.

"That man." Ashley pointed to the picture of a handsome man with prematurely silver hair and a black mustache on the cover of *Tech Times*. "I've seen him before."

Mark glanced at the magazine. "That's Dominic Baldini. He's our chief rival, the one I was concerned was getting information from someone at MarleyHolmes. He's part of what Ed was probing."

"Bette had dinner with him last night over in Breckenridge." Ashley swallowed the bitter taste in her mouth. "Considering they're supposed to be rivals, they were awfully friendly."

22

After Ashley told them about seeing Bette and Dominic Baldini at El Gato Rojo, Kristin shook her head in disbelief. "I thought she might be seeing someone—she had that glow—but she didn't talk about it, so I didn't ask. She's a grown woman who's allowed secrets." She gazed sadly at Baldini's picture. "No wonder she didn't tell me."

Oliver rubbed his hands together. "She's dating your competition. She poisons Ed in a quick replacement for you, Holmes. When either the police labs or my people break Ed's passcode, I bet we'll find evidence he'd collected that point to her as the leak."

"Here's something strange." Ashley told them about the night her printer self-activated and spit out pages of code. "And the label was for Baldini Technologies. At that time, I'd never heard of him or his company."

"But who was sending something to him?" Kristin asked. "And why was it on your printer?"

Ashley shrugged and shook her head. "If it was Bette, here's the irony. I went to her the next day because I was afraid the code was important proprietary information that was being leaked somehow. She assured me it was code for the label. I think she was telling the truth because Chaz Romaine thought so too."

Mark frowned. "How does Chaz fit into this mess?"

"I bumped into him in the hall as I was leaving," Ashley explained. "I gave him all those code papers, and he planned to check into it more."

Mark grabbed his phone. "I'm calling him."

Oliver prowled the room while they waited for Chaz to answer.

"I'm putting you on speaker, Chaz," Mark said, then tapped his phone screen and held out the device. "Tell me what you know about the code and label Dr. Hart gave you."

"Well," Chaz said. "I've checked and rechecked my work, but I come up with the same thing every time. The label was generated from the computer of one of my people."

"Someone at MarleyHolmes?" Mark was stating the obvious, likely because he didn't want to believe it. "Who?"

Chaz hesitated. "Emmett Yancy."

Ashley gasped. "Billy Boy's owner? I can't believe it."

"I can't either," Chaz said. "He's a good guy, but that's not why I don't think he's a sellout. He doesn't have access to enough material to make him anybody's asset. He's not the guy you'd turn if you wanted an insider. You'd pick someone higher up the knowledge chain—you know what I mean?"

"So you're saying someone used his computer?" Oliver had stopped pacing to listen.

"That would be my guess," Chaz said.

"How did the code and label end up on Dr. Hart's printer, Chaz?" Mark asked.

"My best guess is that someone specifically sent it to Dr. Hart's wireless printer with the intention of retrieving it at some point." Chaz hesitated, leaving unsaid the possibility that someone must have planned to break into her house to access the printout.

Ashley snapped her fingers. "Bette said she missed Billy Boy's visit on Friday because she was on a call. She could have made the label while everyone was distracted in the cafeteria. And she stopped by my house with me before we went to lunch Saturday, the day the label printed. Wanting to avoid creating a digital trail by printing it at her own house, she could have tried to print it while she was there. I guess she had trouble with my printer, though."

"The file may have been corrupted," Chaz said. "That would explain why it took until evening to print, and why it spit out all that code."

Mark, who had become contemplative, circled back on his earlier line of questioning. "You're high up the knowledge chain, Chaz."

Talk about blunt. There was a beat of silence, then Chaz said, "I am. But I'm not the only one."

Mark nodded. "No, you're not. Don't mention this to anyone, Chaz. Not a soul."

"I won't." Chaz ended the call.

Mark studied the phone for a long moment, then spoke to Oliver. "Chaz has been with MarleyHolmes almost as long as Bette. I've been keeping an eye on both of them for some time. Back when Clint first hired me, Baldini released a new product so like one we still had in development that it couldn't be coincidence. I've been terrified of the same thing happening again with this new product, and it looks like I'm not paranoid after all."

"But why?" Kristin's voice was raw with betrayal. "After all that Dad did for her, after all we've meant to each other, why?"

Ashley had some ideas about that, but Kristin had been battered enough for one day.

"I'll tell you what I think." Apparently Oliver didn't share Ashley's reservations. "I think she wants power." He paused in front of Mark. "Was she surprised when Clint Marley brought you in?"

Mark shrugged. "I don't know. Then again, she wouldn't have told me. And she wouldn't have told Clint either."

"When she saw Dad's plans for retirement developing, she expected he would name her as his replacement," Kristin murmured, as if she were speaking to herself rather than the group. "He'd brought her along as the company grew, giving her more and more responsibility. In her mind, she was the logical successor. She used to joke about changes she'd make."

"And Clint brought me in over her." Mark rubbed his chin. "No wonder she never liked me."

"She was hurt," Kristin explained. "At least that's what I thought. I was proud of her for being a good team player for the sake of the company. Perhaps I projected how I would have felt on to her. Maybe she was furious. She felt betrayed, so she started plotting to take the company down."

"That might explain that cup of coffee aimed at me," Mark said, "But why wait until now? I've been here for four years."

Oliver shrugged. "Baldini? The new product? Who knows?"

One thing was clear to Ashley: Bette wanted what wasn't hers and had been doing whatever she felt she needed to do to get it. Ashley's gaze rested on Kristin and Mark, seated close together on the couch, and unease prickled her spine. Was it possible Bette wanted more than simply to be in charge of MarleyHolmes?

According to Ellen, Bette had liked Larkin before he met Kristin, yet he'd married Kristin. Had Bette held a torch for Kristin's late husband even after the marriage? Did she harbor jealousy of her best friend's family, thinking it should be hers? She seemed very attached to Garrett.

When Larkin died, Bette had been the wonderful friend who was there in the hour of need. Had Bette the schemer thought her show of concern for Kristin would improve Clint's opinion of her and increase her chances of sitting in the CEO chair?

Then Mark the usurper had shown up. He had taken the business and Kristin's attention. Murdering him would be a way to get revenge against Kristin for . . . what, exactly? Living happily?

The doorbell rang, making them all jump. Kristin stood. "I'll get rid of whoever that is." She disappeared down the hall, and then they heard her exclaim, "Bette! This is an unexpected visit."

"Hey, Kris." Bette's voice was bright and friendly. "Just here to check on Mark. And I brought his favorite Mountain Goat order."

Coffee again? It was a recurring theme with Bette.

Ashley looked from Mark to Oliver. Mark was clearly unhappy, but to Ashley's surprise Ridley grinned. He tapped Ashley on the arm and pointed toward the closed door that led to Mark and Kristin's private quarters. He opened the door and waved for Ashley to follow him. When she hesitated, he took her arm and gently pulled her into the sitting room. Before he closed the door almost entirely, he snapped to get Mark's attention and put his finger to his lips.

Mark nodded and picked up his ginger ale, adopting the role of lonely recovering invalid.

Bette and Kristin walked into the living room.

Bette proffered the coffee. "Got a present for you, Boss."

"Sorry, Bette." Kristin's face gave away nothing. Her acting was impressive. "He can't drink it yet. You know how anesthesia makes things taste strange for a couple of days. He's strictly on ginger ale right now."

"What?" Bette pouted. "Oh no. I had them fix it just the way you like it, Mark."

Ashley gave a little snort at the disingenuous tone in Bette's voice, and Oliver frowned at her. She put her hand to her lips. "Sorry," she whispered.

"Anything new with the rollout?" Mark asked.

Bette gave a brittle little laugh. "Hate to tell you, but we're limping along without you. Take all the time you need to heal."

Mark took a nonchalant sip of his ginger ale. "Security's tight?"

"It couldn't be tighter," Bette said. "I'm keeping an eye on Chaz.

If there is a leak, he's the logical source. He's the only one who knows everything about the new program."

What a neat little piece of character assassination that was, like using Emmett's computer to throw suspicion his way. Ashley felt a chill at Bette's calculation and slid her hands into her jeans pockets as if to warm them. Her fingers encountered something she'd forgotten all about. She withdrew a stained paper towel and held it up.

Oliver raised his eyebrows in question.

"Bette made me coffee this morning," she whispered.

His face furrowed in thought, and he leaned in. "Does she know you saw her last night?"

She shrugged. "I didn't think so, but maybe she saw us—we weren't quiet—and didn't want to acknowledge me any more than I wanted to acknowledge her since she was with a married man."

The more Ashley thought about it, the more she knew something wasn't right about the whole Patch situation. Bette never wanted a kitten. He'd merely been the device to get Ashley to have a cup of coffee. With a shudder, she wondered how she'd be feeling right now if it weren't for Patch's mischief. If she'd be feeling anything at all.

But was being seen with the enemy who happened to be another woman's husband motive for murder? Surely there had to be more?

And she knew.

Danesle see skits.

But it wasn't *Dane*. It was *DeVane*. Ed Warner had been trying to tell her something about Bette.

Ashley ran the words over and over in her mind until suddenly it clicked.

She pulled the door open and strode into the living room. She was vaguely aware of Oliver grabbing at her, but she stormed past him. Bette, Mark, and Kristin turned surprised faces toward her.

She glared at Bette. "Danesle see skits."

Bette blanched. She'd figured it out too. There was the true motive.

"What?" Oliver stared at her, then at Bette.

Ashley crossed her arms. "DeVane sells secrets."

23

For the first time since Ashley had met Bette, the woman seemed unnerved.

"Me?" Wide-eyed, Bette laid a hand on her chest as though she couldn't believe what she was hearing. "Sell secrets? Never! I've poured my life into MarleyHolmes." She issued a short laugh. "Besides, who would I sell them to?"

"How about Dominic Baldini?" Ashley said. "I saw you with him last night at El Gato Rojo. You don't mind that he's married?"

Bette blinked several times, but before she could say anything, the doorbell rang again.

"Who is it this time?" Kristin went to the door while everyone else waited silently. She returned with Chief Maloney.

He scanned the room. "Just the people I wanted to see."

Bette took a step toward the hallway leading to the back door.

"Did you see the kids, Chief?" Ashley asked.

"I did," the chief said. "They were very helpful. They decided to stop at Mountain Goat Coffee to celebrate their sterling detective work. I assume you've all seen their discovery?"

Everyone nodded except Bette. She took another step.

"It's funny, Ms. DeVane." Chief Maloney smiled at Bette, but Ashley thought it was the smile of a fox circling a henhouse. "You were going to be my next stop. How convenient to see you here."

Bette made some sort of inarticulate noise, a cross between panic and bravado.

"I've just been at Eagle's Nest Gifts talking with Marylouise Decker about all the Navajo pottery she's been selling," Chief Maloney went on.

Whatever Bette had been expecting, it wasn't this. "Beautiful, isn't it?" She slid her hands casually into her pockets, but her back was rigid. "And crafted by such a wonderful organization."

"Very pretty," Oliver put in. "Too bad it's not authentic."

The chief shot Oliver a frown. The investigator held up a hand and took a step back.

Maloney turned his attention back to Bette. "You told Marylouise it was the real deal. Margaret White Bear, the great Navajo potter, and her studio full of apprentices."

"Yes," Bette said. "You can find their site online."

The chief nodded. "But there is no potter named Margaret White Bear, Navajo or not, is there?"

Bette frowned. "Of course there is. Isn't there?" She sounded uncertain.

Ashley pictured the room full of boxes and asked the first question that came to mind. "You're behind it, aren't you?" Everyone in the room stared at Ashley. She swallowed. "Patch and I visited Bette this morning, and Patch went investigating. He got into the room full of boxes of pottery."

"You were searching my house?" Bette acted appalled, but her knuckles were white as she clenched her hands. She was more furious than aghast, if Ashley had to guess.

"What are you talking about, Dr. Hart?" the chief asked, and Ashley explained about the morning's adventure. The chief studied Bette as he listened. When the story was done, he said, "I think we need to talk about this more, Ms. DeVane."

Oliver gazed at Bette speculatively. "My firm has done lots of work with counterfeit art, especially Native American art, Chief. We'd be happy to assist you."

The chief nodded. "If there's an illegal ring here, we will find it." He cleared his throat. "But I have bigger concerns too. The state police lab finally broke the encryption on Ed Warner's thumb drive."

Ashley glanced at Bette, but the other woman didn't seem to realize the importance of the drive. Bette merely looked at the chief blankly and took another step.

The chief adopted that fox-like smile again. "Ms. DeVane, they uncovered evidence Ed Warner had gathered against you."

"Against me?" Bette yelped.

"DeVane sells secrets," Ashley repeated.

The chief nodded. "So it appears."

"There's also a little matter of murder, Chief," Mark said. "We need to tell you exactly what we saw on that video that confirms who poisoned Ed Warner."

The back door opened and slammed shut. The kids were home. They must have stopped by the whelping room because, a few moments later, Sweetie ran to Kristin, ears flopping. Kristin picked her up and buried her face in the soft fur.

The three kids bounced into the room, energized by achievement and coffee.

"Mom, you won't believe—" Rani came to an abrupt halt when she saw Bette.

Garrett glared at Bette with eyes full of distress and sorrow. "Aunt Bette, how—" His voice broke. "How could you?"

Bette stared back. "How could I what?"

"We have a video of you putting the cup in the trash bag," Garrett managed. "I finally figured it out the eighth time we watched it."

Bette blinked at that news. She had to know what cup and what bag Garrett was talking about. They were the only cup and bag that mattered.

"Of course I put an empty cup in the trash," Bette argued brazenly. "That's where you put things like that."

"We can see the bandage from your carpal tunnel surgery," Garrett told her.

Bette smiled. "What does it matter? That bag and that cup are at the dump."

"But this isn't at the dump." Ashley reached into her pocket and pulled out the stained paper towel she'd used that morning. "I used this to clean up the coffee you served me this morning. What do you think the police will find when they test it? Maybe some tetrodotoxin?"

"Ms. DeVane, I think we have a lot to talk about," Chief Maloney said. "Would you accompany me downtown?"

When he spoke, Bette spun toward the back hall and tried to make a run for it.

Ashley, who'd been watching the woman's incremental retreat, took a step of her own to block her path. "You can't run away from this, Bette." Ashley crossed her arms. "It's over."

24

Ashley brushed the snow off her coat and draped it over the back of her chair at Miss Abigale's Tea Room. She took the fourth seat at the table, between Ellen and Kristin and across from Holly. Evergreen garlands and potted poinsettias had replaced the pumpkins and leaves that had decorated the tearoom when Ashley had come with Bette. Nearly a month had passed since Bette DeVane's arrest, and the rest of Aspen Falls had carried on without her.

Ellen fluffed her hair, flattened by her hat. "Well, Bette was top of the news on the Denver stations again this morning. She's accused of involvement in a ring selling counterfeit Navajo pottery throughout the West."

"Is it wrong that I still like my turtle?" Ashley laid her napkin in her lap. "He's so cute."

Holly shot her a sympathetic glance. "I love mine too. I think it's okay for us to keep them." Her smile turned wry. "They're quite a souvenir of the last few weeks."

"I'm surprised Bette had the time to put into yet another illegal enterprise," Ellen said.

Kristin cringed. "Based on what I've put together, she was funneling the charitable donations MarleyHolmes contributes every year into a fake non-profit organization she claimed was supporting Native American women artisans. The money was really going into her own account and she was selling fakes made overseas for a fraction of what she charged for them."

"Just one more way to cheat MarleyHolmes, sounds like," Holly said. "So what's her crime tally now? I count murder, attempted murder, corporate espionage, and fraud."

"Dallying with a married man isn't a crime, but it should be," Ellen said with a sniff.

Kristin shook her head. "She wasn't actually seeing Dominic Baldini, although they were certainly thick as thieves over ruining MarleyHolmes. Bette was probably banking on making enough money to continue her lifestyle with her other ventures. That is, if she wasn't planning to get a different corporate job, possibly at Baldini Tech."

"Is Baldini going to jail?" Ashley asked. "He was buying the secrets Bette was selling, after all."

"I hear they're working on a criminal case," Holly put in. "But either way, his reputation in the business world is ruined. Baldini Tech stocks have tanked and he's being forced out as CEO."

A server arrived and they ordered the afternoon tea for four, then Ellen said, "Whatever criminal case they build against him, I bet the information on that thumb drive will be at the heart of it."

"How did it get into the kittens' basket left on your steps, Ashley?" Holly asked. "I've been wondering that."

"Henry." Kristin shook her head. "He was in the house to get the basket and fabric for the kittens. As he left the house to go back to the barn, he passed Ed Warner in the back hall. Warner was leaving after brunch. My best guess is that he was starting to feel the tetrodotoxin and wanted to put the drive somewhere safe after he ran into Bette."

Their server returned with their first platter of tea sandwiches, and Ellen, Holly, and Ashley oohed and ahhed over the pretty little triangles. While the others served themselves, though, Kristin sat back, her shoulders slumped.

"Are you okay, Kristin?" Ashley asked, then realized what must be bothering her friend. "Are you remembering coming here with Bette?"

Kristin nodded. "We ate here all the time. I had no idea she was so bitter, so jealous of my life." She gave a mirthless laugh. "I feel so duped."

"Oh, Kristin." Ashley abandoned the serving spatula and reached for Kristin's hand. "It's better to be deceived than to be a deceiver. You are kind and tenderhearted. Sure, trusting opens you to being used, but you've still got everything you had before all this happened—"

"Except a best friend." Kristin made a face.

Ashley tipped her head in acknowledgment. "But she's got nothing. All her scheming and manipulation and nothing. You've not only got your friends"—she indicated those at the table, who all nodded agreement—"but you've also got your reputation, your ethics, and your family."

"Trusting is a risk," Holly agreed. "It does leave you vulnerable, but can you imagine always manipulating, conniving, scheming?" She shuddered. "I'd rather trust until I learn otherwise."

"I don't know," Kristin said. "Trusting sure has gotten me into some trouble."

Ashley offered Kristin an encouraging smile. "Consider Henry, though. You chose to take a chance on him, to trust you could make a difference."

Kristin's expression brightened. "You should see him and that kitten. Even Rani said they were made for each other. He's still got lots of rough edges, but we have hope."

"And you trusted Garrett to find his way." Ellen tipped her teacup in Kristin's direction. "He's found his calling with horses, just like his father, and now he's got new goals and dreams for his life and career. Sure, it took time, but you gave it to him."

"And don't forget," Holly added, "your caring, trusting nature is what attracted two wonderful men, Larkin and Mark."

Kristin looked from woman to woman. "I didn't want to come today—no offense intended."

Ashley smiled. "None taken. I had guessed as much."

"Mark encouraged me to," Kristin continued. "He told me I had to stop focusing on what I lost and remember what I had. He was right. I'm so glad I came."

"So are we," Holly said, raising her teacup. "Here's to real friendship."

"Hear, hear!" they all chorused, lifting their cups to toast. Ashley felt her heart swell. There really was nothing like true friends.